COVER SIX
SECURITY

Lisa B. Kamps

COVERED by a kiss

A COVER SIX SECURITY NOVELLA

USA Today Bestselling Author
LISA B. KAMPS

COVERED BY A KISS

Covered By A Kiss
Copyright © 2019 by Elizabeth Belbot Kamps

All rights reserved. Except for use in any review, the reproduction or utilization of this work in whole or in part in any form by any electronic, mechanical or other means, now known or hereafter invented, including xerography, photocopying and recording, or in any information storage or retrieval system, is forbidden without the express written permission of the author.

Cover Six Security™ is a fictional security company, its name and logo created for the sole use of the author and covered under protection of trademark.

All characters in this book have no existence outside the imagination of the author and have no relation to anyone bearing the same name or names, living or dead. This book is a work of fiction and any resemblance to any individual, place, business, or event is purely coincidental.

Cover Design by Dark Water Covers
https://www.facebook.com/darkwatercovers/

Cover Six Security Logo Designed by Benjamin Mangnus of Benjamagnus Design Ltd.
http://www.benjamagnus.com/

All rights reserved.

contents

Copyright iv
Other titles by this author vii
Chapter One 9
Chapter Two 17
Chapter Three 23
Chapter Four 28
Chapter Five 33
Chapter Six 37
Chapter Seven 46
Chapter Eight 52
Chapter Nine 60
Chapter Ten 69
Chapter Eleven 74
Chapter Twelve 80
Chapter Thirteen 85
Chapter Fourteen 91
Chapter Fifteen 98
The Protector: MAC 103
The Guardian: DARYL 107
The Defender: RYDER 108
About the Author 109

Lisa B. Kamps

Other titles by this author

COVER SIX SECURITY

Covered By A Kiss, A CSS Novella, Book 0
The Protector: MAC, Book 1
The Guardian: DARYL, Book 2
The Defender: RYDER, Book 3

THE BALTIMORE BANNERS

Crossing The Line, Book 1
Game Over, Book 2
Blue Ribbon Summer, Book 3
Body Check, Book 4
Break Away, Book 5
Playmaker (A Baltimore Banners Intermission novella)
Delay of Game, Book 6
Shoot Out, Book 7
The Baltimore Banners 1st Period Trilogy (Books 1-3)
The Baltimore Banners 2nd Period Trilogy (Books 4-6)
On Thin Ice, Book 8
Coach's Challenge (A Baltimore Banners Intermission Novella)
One-Timer, Book 9
Face Off, Book 10
First Shot At Love (A Baltimore Banners Warm-up Story)
Game Misconduct, Book 11
Fighting To Score, Book 12
Matching Penalties, Book 13

THE YORK BOMBERS

Playing The Game, Book 1

Playing To Win, Book 2
Playing For Keeps, Book 3
Playing It Up, Book 4
Playing It Safe, Book 5
Playing For Love, Book 6
Playing His Part, Book 7

THE CHESAPEAKE BLADES

Winning Hard, Book 1
Loving Hard, Book 2
Playing Hard, Book 3

FIREHOUSE FOURTEEN

Once Burned, Book 1
Playing With Fire, Book 2
Breaking Protocol, Book 3
Into The Flames, Book 4
Second Alarm, Book 5

STAND-ALONE TITLES

Emeralds and Gold: A Treasury of Irish Short Stories *(anthology)*
Finding Dr. Right, Silhouette Special Edition
Time To Heal
Dangerous Passion

chapter ONE

Nothing was the way she remembered it. Not even close.

Tabitha "TR" Meyers stood just inside the main entranceway, her gaze sweeping around the interior. The heavy door closed behind her, startling her, and she took another step inside.

The door was new. And so was the entranceway. Or maybe she should call it what it was: a small lobby. Complete with dark grey carpet, stiff chairs upholstered in a lighter grey, and even a large receptionist desk along the back wall. A tiny little Christmas tree, lonely and pathetic, was placed at the corner of the desk.

The tree appeared even smaller next to the huge guy leaning against the desk—and he didn't look like any receptionist she had ever seen before. Tall, with broad shoulders nearly ripping the seams from the body-hugging black t-shirt he wore. Arms the size of her thighs and covered in dark ink folded across a wide chest. He had dark hair, clipped short on the sides, a little longer on top. Equally dark eyes watched her, their depths void of all emotion. Not cold, not exactly...but a chill still teased her spine.

Maybe it wasn't the eyes that caused the chill. Maybe it was the sight of the large weapon casually tucked into a worn leather shoulder holster that made her take an involuntary step back.

No, it wasn't that, either—although the man and the weapon were both intimidating, by themselves *and* coupled together as they were. The chill had nothing to do with the man. Or the weapon. Or even with the way everything around her had changed since the last time she'd been here.

The icy shivers skating along her spine were a direct result of the reason *why* she was here. Not for the first time, she questioned the wisdom of coming here. Questioned her sanity. Wondered if she had any idea at all about what she was getting herself into simply by walking through that front door.

None of that mattered. Not now, not when her mind was made up. She was on a mission. Maybe it was a foolish one, but she couldn't back away now.

The man stared at her for another long minute, his dark gaze penetrating. Sizing her up. Determining if she presented any danger. TR almost laughed at that. Dangerous? Her? Only if she had a pen in her hand—

And only if she could verify that cryptic email she had received two weeks ago.

The guy finally straightened to his full height and dropped his arms to his sides. His gaze still didn't waver, even if one eyebrow lifted just the smallest bit when he addressed her.

"Is there something you need?"

TR blinked in surprise. She had expected a gravelly voice, rough and maybe even a bit harsh. She certainly hadn't expected the deceptively smooth warmth that caressed her. She had no idea who the man was—he hadn't been here the last time she'd been here, almost a year ago. None of this had been here. The place had been little more than an old warehouse, large and empty and filled with nothing more than possibilities and a few locked storage lockers.

Panic nipped at her. Had anything else changed? Maybe the man she'd come to see wasn't even here. Maybe he'd moved on. Maybe something had happened to him—

TR swallowed back that last thought, swallowed back the panic and doubt. She would have heard, would have known somehow—

The guy was still staring at her, those dark eyes piercing through her unaccustomed spurt of panic. TR cleared her throat and pasted a large smile on her face, hoping it hid the whirlwind of emotion battering her insides.

"Is Gordon here?"

The man's chiseled face transformed from a mask of indifference to a confused frown. He shook his head, the slight motion filling TR with disappointment. "There's nobody here by that name."

TR's smile faltered. No. That wasn't right. He had to be here. TR forced the smile back into place and asked again. "Gordon MacGregor? Mac? He doesn't work here?"

"Oh. Mac." The frown lifted from the man's face as some of the wariness left his stiff body. "Yeah, he's here. You need him?"

Need. Such a strong word. Did she need Mac? She had once prided herself on never needing anyone—but not now. Not for this. Yes, she needed Mac.

But that wasn't what the man meant, not in that way.

TR gave herself a mental shake and forced another smile. "Yes. Please."

A brief flash of surprise crossed the man's face, then quickly disappeared with a low grunt. He moved behind the desk and grabbed the phone, started punching at numbers with the blunt tip of one long finger. He held the receiver to his ear, frowning as he kept stabbing buttons.

TR bit back a real smile when the man cursed and slammed the receiver down. He shot a dark glance in her direction then moved away from the desk toward a door several feet away.

"Standby." The command came out as a growl tossed over his shoulder. He moved to the side, hiding the keypad from her view as he punched in a long string of numbers. TR had just enough time to wonder why they needed the extra security when the man pushed the heavy door open and stuck his head inside—and bellowed.

"Yo. Mac. Company."

TR winced at the loud shout then jumped in guilt when she realized the man had noticed. He slammed the door shut then stood off to the side, his arms once more crossed in front of his wide chest.

A minute later, the door swung open again. The breath froze in her lungs as another man stepped out. Just as large. Just as intimidating. Maybe even more so because of the scowl twisting his scarred face.

One heartbeat went by, then another and another,

ticking away the seconds as her pulse sped up. It had been nearly a year since she'd last seen him, and he hadn't changed a bit.

No, that wasn't true. He seemed larger than she remembered. Broader. A little harder. His hair was a bit longer and that wide jaw was covered in dark scruff, like he hadn't bothered to shave for a few days. The scruff wasn't even, the dark stubble broken by the scars covering the lower half of his face.

TR dropped her gaze, taking a much-needed few seconds to recover from the powerful impact of seeing him again. Damn him. He shouldn't have this effect on her, shouldn't be able to make her pulse race and her breath hitch in her chest. Not after what he'd said, not after he'd made it perfectly clear there could be nothing between them.

Not after he'd made it perfectly clear he wanted to be nothing more than friends.

Had he seen her yet? Noticed her standing there in the middle of the room? TR risked a glance upward then bit back a sigh. No, he hadn't seen her. He was too busy scowling at the other man.

"What the fuck, Boomer? You can't use the fucking intercom?"

Maybe this was a bad idea. No, it *was* a bad idea, TR had known that from the beginning. But she was desperate, had thought that maybe—

"The damn thing doesn't work. Zeus needs to get off his ass and hire someone because this secretary shit fucking sucks."

"Yeah. You go right ahead and tell him that."

TR took a small step backward, then another. Maybe she could sneak out, just go back to her office and rethink things. There had to be another way. Other options she wasn't seeing. Her hand closed around the door handle, the cold metal somehow reassuring. She started to turn it, mere steps away from escaping and making what she now knew was a mistake—

"TR. Freeze."

The command surprised her so thoroughly that she did exactly that—froze in place, one foot hovering several inches off the ground, the knob paused halfway in its turn. A pair of dark eyes impaled her, holding her prisoner with the intensity of their gaze.

How long did she stay that way, frozen mid-step, her heart slamming against her chest as guilt raced through her? She felt like a small child caught in the middle of doing something wrong, knowing that punishment was about to be meted out.

It was a ridiculous feeling, one that ignited a small flash of temper. The temper fizzed out faster than it appeared, replaced by something even worse as Mac held her gaze.

Attraction. Need. Desire.

And damn him. How could he make those unwanted feelings appear with nothing more than his intense gaze? It wasn't even a warm gaze. There was no appreciation in the depths of his eyes, no desire or regret or even welcome. Just steely impartiality as he stared at her.

Watching her.

Sizing her up.

That brief flash of temper resurfaced, just long enough for her to regain an ounce of composure. She lowered her foot to the floor and released her death grip on the doorknob, wishing she could pull her gaze away from Mac.

She couldn't, no more than she could make herself

walk back out the door.

Mac shifted, just the tiniest bit, his solid weight moving from one booted foot to the other. He didn't turn his head, didn't look away, just issued a quiet command in that rough voice of his.

"Boomer. Get lost."

"But—"

"Now."

There was no mistaking the finality of the command. The other man—was his name really Boomer?—simply turned and disappeared down the hallway to the right. There was no sound of retreating footsteps, no low-pitched muttering. Just an eerie silence that would have made a shiver of apprehension skitter along her spine—

If a shiver of another kind hadn't already appeared, prickling her skin with awareness.

TR finally blinked, forced her gaze away from Mac's and stared at the floor. Air filled her lungs and she absently wondered if she had been holding her breath the entire time. Yes, she had—much like she was doing now as Mac's long legs ate up the distance between them. He stopped less than a foot away, his solid bulk both comforting and intimidating. TR tilted her head back, her gaze focused on the uneven stubble covering his chiseled jaw. She couldn't meet his gaze, not again. If she did, she'd end up doing something foolish—and she was tired of making a fool of herself in front of this man.

"TR."

That was it, just her name in his low, rough voice. But there was something else there, too, a hint of warmth that surprised her enough to look up and meet his gaze.

It was the worst thing she could do. She felt her resolve slipping under the weight of those dark eyes, felt herself drowning in their depths. She was going to do something foolish, she knew it.

No. No, she wouldn't. She *couldn't*.

But he was still watching her, holding her prisoner with nothing more than a look. "What are you doing here, TR?"

She started to shake her head, tried to bite down on the words, but it was too late. They fell from her lips with no thought to why she had come here in the first place, with no care for what she needed to do.

And with no finesse whatsoever.

"I need a date."

chapter TWO

I need a date.

The words surprised him almost as much as seeing TR standing in the lobby. He didn't know what the hell she was doing here, and he sure as hell hadn't expected to see her when he walked through the door.

But she was here, and he *had* seen her—had been aware of her on a level he didn't understand even before he'd closed the door behind him. He hadn't looked over at her, had busied himself by giving Boomer shit because if he looked at her, he might do something totally out of character for him, like walk over and pull her into a hug.

And fuck, he still wanted to do that. Maybe more now than a few minutes ago because he was closer to her now, so close he could feel the heat of her body across the short distance separating him, so close he could smell the sweet fruitiness of her shampoo. Not perfume—TR didn't wear it. But she still carried a scent that was uniquely her and—

Fuck. What the hell was he doing? Was he actually leaning forward, ready to sniff her? He needed his fucking head examined.

No. What he needed was a stiff drink, a shower, and about twelve hours of sleep—not necessarily in that order. They'd just returned from an op that should have been a cakewalk, only it had turned into huge clusterfuck. How the hell did you rescue someone who didn't want to be rescued? Who had disappeared on purpose with her lowlife pond scum of a boyfriend simply because Daddy didn't approve?

Fuck it. That was Daryl's problem now, not his. His only problem was going home to wash off the funk that had accumulated after five days of bullshit.

No, belay that. His first problem was getting rid of TR. Then he could go home and take care of everything else.

Only he didn't want to get rid of TR and that was an even bigger problem. He'd walked away from her almost a year ago. Walked? Hell, he practically *ran* away from her, right after telling her they could only be friends.

And wasn't that a fucking kick in the ass? It was probably one of the biggest lies that had ever crossed his lips—and one of the hardest fucking things he'd ever had to do. Friends? Christ. Not even close.

But no way in fucking hell could he let anything happen between them. She deserved more—one hell of a lot more. He had nothing to offer her, nothing except a scarred body that had stood on the edges of hell more times than he cared to count.

TR deserved more—only she didn't see it that way. She didn't see *him* that way. She didn't see him for what he really was: a scarred, battle-worn soldier who was too rough around the edges for civilian life. Or maybe she *did* see him for what he was and simply didn't care.

And that made her dangerous.

The irony wasn't lost on him. Of all the fucking shit he'd seen, all the fucking shit he'd done, it was the woman standing in front of him that scared him the most.

Not that he'd ever admit that out loud. Hell, no. He didn't have to, either—at least, not to Daryl Anderson and Jonathan Riegler, his partners at Cover Six Security. They both knew exactly what TR did to him—and they both made it a point of letting him know what they thought of his evade-and-escape tactic almost a year ago.

It was the thought of either one of them stepping out into this plush lobby that prompted him to wrap his hand around TR's arm and tug her toward the hallway. She followed him—for two steps. Then she dug her heels in and refused to budge.

Not that he couldn't move her if he wanted to—she was a tiny thing, with more sass than size. It would be nothing to throw her over his shoulder and haul her off—

He damn near laughed at the idea. Yeah, he could go all fucking caveman on her—if he relished the idea of having his balls kicked up to his throat. TR would do it, too, of that he had no doubt.

One glance at her made him wonder if she was already considering doing just that. Her chin was lifted in a defiant tilt that sent her thick black hair cascading down her back. And those clear eyes of her, so blue they matched a summer sky, sparked with some kind of emotion. Impatience? Irritation? A silent dare?

Hell if he knew. But he was smart enough to drop his hand and take a step back.

I need a date.

What the fuck did that even mean? Why was she here, after he'd done his best to scare her off all those months ago?

Mac opened his mouth, ready to ask that exact question, when she placed one fist on her denim-clad hip and narrowed her eyes at him.

"Where are you taking me?"

He sucked in a deep breath, mentally counted to three to control his voice, then narrowed his own eyes. "I was going to take you back to my office but if you'd rather have this discussion here—"

"No, your office is fine." Her gaze darted to the side, just for a split-second, and he had the impression she was trying to hide a flash of disappointment. What the fuck she had to be disappointed about was beyond him. He didn't bother to question her, just simply turned and headed down the hallway without a word, knowing from the sound of her footsteps that she was following him. He shortened the length of his strides, not wanting to get too far ahead of her. If he did, she'd never find her way through the dizzying maze of hallways and doors.

He finally reached his office and pushed open the door, standing to the side so TR could enter in front of him. She brushed past him then hesitated, her body flinching as the door closed with a soft click. Mac tamped down the desire to reassure her and stepped over to his desk, lowering his bulky weight into the chair and shifting to get comfortable.

TR's gaze scanned the small room. He briefly

wondered what she'd been expecting. A well-lit corner office with a view? A room decorated with expensive accents designed to impress? Not fucking likely, not in their line of work. The computer system on the work station behind him was state-of-the-art but everything else was bare-bones functional. The desk, the two chairs, the filing cabinet he had accidentally dented the first week he'd had it—they were there to serve a purpose and nothing else. There were no windows, no potted plants, no personal touches at all—unless you counted his go-bag tossed in the corner where he'd dropped it thirty minutes ago.

He waited another minute, watching TR as she continued to study the office before finally settling in the stiff-backed chair across from him. Silence filled the room, heavy with expectancy, tight with tension. His? Hers? Maybe a little of both.

He leaned back in the chair, his gaze giving nothing away as he watched her.

The silky thickness of her black hair. The way the long strands clung to her fingers when she pushed a thick hank behind her ear. The sparkle of light as it hit her earring, reflecting back at him with flashes of red and orange and blue. The way the fringed hem of her long sweater clung to her thigh as she shifted in the chair. The glimpse of creamy flesh peeking from the V-neck of the linen blouse.

He swallowed and dropped his gaze, watching as she crossed her long legs. The whisper of leather brushing against leather filled the silence when her boots rubbed against each other as she shifted once more. The impatient sway of her foot was almost hypnotic—back-and-forth, back-and-forth. Restless. Nervous.

And totally at odds with the woman he knew. TR wasn't restless, and she certainly didn't get nervous.

"What do you want, TR?" Did the gruff impatience of his voice bother her? If it did, she didn't let it show. She simply tilted that chin up a notch and met his steady gaze with one of her own.

"You."

chapter THREE

You. I need you.

TR's quiet voice echoed around the small room, the words ringing in his ear with the force of an explosion.

You.

Fuck.

How many times had he dreamed of hearing those words? Too many. But dreams were one thing—reality was something completely different. He didn't deserve to hear them. Not a year ago. Not now.

And *fuck*! Thank God he had a poker face because her answer damn near floored him. It was the last thing he expected to hear her say. From the pale flush staining her cheeks, it was probably the last thing she had expected to say. Her lids fluttered, those dark lashes creating a shadow against her smooth skin. Her foot stopped swaying as she uncrossed her long legs; a dull thud echoed in the quiet room as the heel of her boot connected with the carpeted floor.

"I mean—" She cleared her throat and shot a quick glance in his direction through those fringed eyes. "I want to hire you."

"Hire me."

A flash of temper flared in her clear blue eyes, there and gone before he really had time to register it. "Yes. Hire you."

"For what?"

"I told you: I need a date."

"Tabitha—"

"Don't call me that. You know I hate that name."

Yeah, he did—which was why he used it. Better to have her get pissed and storm off before he did something fucking stupid. "Tabitha, this isn't an escort service—"

"I know that—"

"It's a security service specializing in high-risk operations—"

"I know that. I still want to hire—"

"You can't afford me. Us."

Her pale eyes heated with another flash of anger, this one lasting more than a few seconds. She leaned forward and placed one hand on the edge of his desk, her fingers tightening until the knuckles turned white. Mac was positive she was pretending the desk was his neck, and that she was happily strangling him in her mind.

He didn't move, didn't blink, didn't breathe. He just sat there watching her, waiting to see what she would do next.

Hoping she would simply get up and leave. What would he do then? Would he go after her, or let her walk out?

He'd let her walk out, just like he'd done nearly a year ago. Let her? Hell, he'd practically tossed her out the door, wounding her pride just enough to make sure she never came back. She deserved more than he could ever give her and that was the only way he knew to cut whatever ties had unexpectedly grown between them.

He was a fucking ass. The fact that he was sitting here, practically doing the same damn thing again, was proof of that.

The heavy silence was finally broken by the small sound TR made—a cross between a growl and a sigh of frustration. She reached into the large purse hanging from her shoulder, her gaze never leaving his.

"Don't you even want to know why I'm asking? Why I would humiliate myself by even coming here?"

Humiliate? He hadn't thought of it that way, hadn't considered how she might feel seeing him again. Hadn't considered what kind of effect coming here would have on her.

He started to ask, thought better of it, then changed his mind and opened his mouth. What should have been a simple question came out as a bellow, the roar echoing off the walls of the small room.

"What the fuck is *that*?"

TR jumped, her surprise clear in the way she flinched. A furious blush stained her cheeks as she tried to push the weapon back into her purse. "It's...nothing."

"Nothing, hell." Mac moved around the desk with a lightning speed that caught her off-guard. He yanked the purse from her hand and reached in, pulling out the shitty peashooter she was probably calling a gun.

He tossed the purse to the desk, his gaze focused on the small Beretta 950 Jetfire. The safety was on, thank God for small miracles. He released the clip and sat it behind him on the desk, then racked the slide to clear the chamber. Empty—another small miracle. The .25 caliber handgun might be a peashooter of a pocket gun, but it could still do damage in the wrong hands.

And TR's feminine hands were definitely the wrong hands.

"Why the fuck do you even have this thing? Are you trying to kill yourself?"

"I have a permit."

She was lying, he could see it in the way her gaze dropped to the desk behind him. He didn't call her out on it, though. He simply moved across the room and placed the empty weapon in the top drawer of the filing cabinet then quietly locked it.

"Hey! That's mine—"

"You don't even know how to use it."

"I do, too. I've taken lessons."

God save him from civilians who had *taken lessons*. Didn't she know how many people were killed with their own handguns each year, because they either didn't know how to use them—or were afraid to use them when the time came? Maybe she did, maybe she didn't. He wasn't going to lecture her, not now. Not until he found out why she felt the need to go around armed.

"What's going on, TR?"

"I told you: I need a date."

Mac swallowed a growl of frustration as he moved toward her. He leaned forward and placed one hand on each arm of the chair, imprisoning her with his size, with his nearness. She sat back, trying to put distance between them, but she had nowhere to go, not when she was trapped in the chair. Her head tilted back, her eyes widening as he leaned in even closer.

"What's going on, TR?" He repeated the question, his voice low and gruff, barely more than a whisper. Her gaze met his and for the briefest second, panic and worry clouded the clear blue of her eyes. Then her chin tilted up just a fraction of an inch, her shoulders stiffening with determination.

"I told you: I need a date. That's it."

chapter **FOUR**

The morning had been a complete failure. TR tried to ignore the disappointment, tried to tell herself it didn't matter. She hadn't really expected Mac to agree. Why would he? Especially after he'd made his position clear all those months ago.

Maybe if she had told him why—

She shook her head, mentally shoving the thought away. Telling him why would just give him another reason to say no and open up the doors to one more lecture. He'd already lectured her on the hazards of carrying a gun illegally—and okay, maybe it was a stupid thing to do. She still wasn't sure why she'd started carrying it, not that it mattered anymore since the thing was now locked up in his office. But she didn't need another lecture from him and that's what he'd give her if she told him why she needed a date—only this time, the lecture would be on the wisdom of getting involved in something that was nothing more than a wild goose chase.

But what if it wasn't a wild goose chase? What if there really was something to the email she'd received?

TR clicked open the tab for her email program then quickly scrolled through the folders, finally choosing the one labeled "Shopping". Misfiling the message wouldn't stop anyone from finding it, not if they were really looking. Her work email was secure—to a point. Her passwords were long and confusing—to a point. But enough to stop anyone who was determined to break into the system?

Not even close.

She wasn't foolish enough—or naive enough—to believe that anything on her computer was even remotely secure. If it was hooked to the internet or stored in a cloud somewhere, it was fair game. Her private files were backed-up and stored offline. Drafts, stories, research, notes, contacts, all of it. The only way anyone could get to those files was by stealing one of her thumb drives—and she had three of them. One was always with her, one was locked up in her home office, and the other was stored here at work.

Paranoid? Maybe just a little. But she'd lost all her work before. Not once, but twice. That would be enough to make anyone paranoid.

Not that anyone would actually steal her stuff. There was nothing to steal. Her stories were mostly human-interest pieces, like the series she had done on the Chesapeake Blades and the new women's hockey league. Not exactly fluff, but not exactly earth-shattering, either.

Which made the email she had received two weeks ago all the more puzzling.

She clicked on it now, frowning as she read it for

what must be the millionth time.

There's more to the new defense complex than you think. Look deeper. Follow the money. Follow your instinct.

TR had no idea what the message meant. The defense complex was nothing more than a new training facility being constructed just outside Frederick, on a sprawling parcel of land that might be in the middle of nowhere but wasn't exactly secluded. The facility was small, hardly large enough to be called a complex, practically inconsequential when compared to other facilities. It wasn't even that important, in the grand scheme of things. She was covering it for a story she was working on, weighing the economic benefits to the area against the destruction of a potentially historic piece of land. It wasn't exactly an earth-shattering story.

So who sent the message? And why? Were they even referring to the same project?

TR had no idea and part of her wondered if maybe she was being pranked. Maybe one of her new co-workers thought it would be funny to pull her into a cloak-and-dagger mystery then sit back and watch her run around chasing her tail.

Maybe.

Then again, maybe not.

Follow your instinct.

TR closed her eyes, tried to empty her mind of everything else and focus on what her gut was telling her. If it was just the email, she'd give it a half-hearted look then let it go. But getting the invitation to the New Year's Eve party five days after receiving the email? A party being hosted by the same Senator who just happened to be the driving force behind the new facility?

The same Senator who had given her the run-around when she initially contacted him for an interview only to suddenly be available *today*? The week between Christmas and New Year's, when Congress wasn't even in session?

That was too much of a coincidence, especially since she had only spoken to the Senator exactly one time before—every other contact had been through his office. One conversation, and suddenly she was being invited to a black-tie affair to ring in the new year?

No, she wasn't buying it. Maybe there was a perfectly reasonable explanation for the invitation. Maybe the Senator's assistant had accidentally added her name to the wrong list. Or maybe the invitation was nothing more than a subtle attempt at bribery: invite the reporter from the small paper to a party. Impress her in the hopes of garnering a favorable review when she wrote the article.

TR snorted, the indelicate sound echoing around her. No, she still wasn't buying it. If the paper was bigger than a regional weekly *and* if she covered local or national politics *and* if she had built her name up for something other than human interest pieces...then *maybe* it might make sense. If the story had even a remotely political slant, then maybe she'd buy it.

But it didn't. Not even close.

So why had she been invited? And who had sent the email? And what the hell did it all mean?

Not going to the party wasn't an option. She'd go alone if she had to but she'd definitely feel more comfortable if someone went with her. That was why she'd finally decided to break down and go see Mac this morning. She could mingle, ask questions, maybe even do a little snooping if Mac was with her. Nobody would think twice of questioning him and she had no doubt he'd keep her safe if she got caught.

But who would keep her safe from him?

She swallowed back a small growl of frustration at the thought. It was a moot point anyway—he'd told her no, in no uncertain terms. She certainly wasn't going to beg him. She'd simply go by herself, no big deal.

TR shoved all thoughts of Mac from her mind and closed out of the programs she had running before shutting the computer down. She'd already wasted too much time—she had the meeting with the Senator in two hours and she'd be lucky to make it to his office on Capitol Hill in time. Traffic into DC was always a nightmare. Maybe she'd have better luck taking 295 instead of I-95.

Or maybe she'd skip the drive altogether and just take the MARC train down. That would probably be the best thing to do. The train ticket and parking at Penn Station would be a lot cheaper than parking anywhere in DC, and she wouldn't have to deal with the headache of driving.

Her mind made up, she grabbed her oversized tote bag and headed into the ladies' restroom to change. It was a small paper and the office dress code was relaxed—as in, almost nonexistent—but no way was she going to meet a US Senator wearing jeans.

Ten minutes later, dressed in tailored black slacks and low-heeled shoes, she was walking out the door. She'd have plenty of time on the train to review the questions she wanted to ask the Senator. And, with any luck, maybe her subconscious would work overtime and figure out what to do about that cryptic email.

And *not* think about the Mac dressed in a tux.

chapter FIVE

He couldn't sleep.

Mac rolled to his side and glanced at the clock with a grunt. He'd managed to doze, but only in fits and starts. Would it be worth it to stay here in bed and try again?

No, it wouldn't. Not when he couldn't shake the feeling that something was about to happen. He tried to tell himself the feeling was nothing more than his imagination, that the subtle uneasiness washing over him had more to do with his surprise visitor this morning than anything else.

Seeing TR had rattled him more than he cared to admit. Not just her visit—that was surprising enough by itself. But for her to show up after nearly a year—

For a fucking *date*.

He didn't buy it this morning, and he wasn't buying it now. A date? Oh hell no. The woman was up to something.

But what?

Maybe that's why he was so uneasy, why he couldn't shake the feeling that something was about to happen. The mere thought of TR being up to something was enough to make the man upstairs shudder with worry. Mac—being a mere mortal—should probably be shaking in his size thirteen boots.

He tossed the covers to the side then rolled to a sitting position on the edge of the bed. Christ, he was getting old if simply laying in bed was enough to make his body stiff. He rolled his head from side-to-side, the vertebrae making loud popping noises that echoed through the silence of the room. His shoulders were next. Up and down. Back then front. Two more times, until some of the tension left the abused muscles.

He reached for the pair of sweatpants tossed across the foot of the bed, stepping into them as he stood up. Barefoot and bare-chested, he made his way to the bathroom to splash cold water on his face—a face he didn't bother to look at in the mirror. He knew how the scars looked, could trace every ragged line with his eyes closed. Some thin and shiny, some thick and twisted, all forming a roadmap of destruction on his lower face. The scars had bothered him at first, which surprised him because he wasn't a particularly vain man. At least, he hadn't thought so, not until he'd seen what a fucking mess his face had become, thanks to one well-placed IED.

But hell, it could have been worse. A lot worse. He was one of the lucky ones from that day—he hadn't woken up dead.

Yeah, real fucking lucky.

He pushed the memories away before they could resurface, dried his face, then headed downstairs to the kitchen and walked straight to the coffee machine. A nice jolt of caffeine would clear the fog in his mind. With any luck, it would work to dispel the lingering uneasiness still clinging to him.

Why the fuck had TR stopped by this morning? That was what kept bothering him: the *why*. Because fuck no, he wasn't buying that whole bullshit about needing a date. She was up to something, he just didn't know what.

Maybe you should have asked her.

Mac frowned then mentally told the voice in his head to shut the fuck up. Yeah, he should have asked her. If it had been anyone else, he *would* have asked. But it was TR and instead of asking, he fucking froze.

Because he was afraid of the answer?

Fuck no. It was because he was afraid he'd say *yes*. And that was the worst fucking thing he could do. TR was his weakness, something he'd finally admitted to himself at the beginning of the year at Jonathan Reigler's wedding. TR had gone with him—and he still had no idea how the fuck it had worked out that way—but it wasn't a *date*.

Not that she hadn't tried to turn it into one. He could still feel the weight of her hand—so damn small and delicate and warm—on his arm as she leaned toward him. Could feel the softness of one small breast press against his chest as she stepped even closer and tilted her head back. Her soft lips had parted and he knew—he fucking *knew*—she was going to kiss him. And Christ, he'd wanted her to, wanted it with a feverish need that still scared the piss right out of him. He wanted to feel her soft lips part beneath his. Wanted to taste the warmth of her mouth, wondered if it would be as sweet as the wine she'd been drinking.

No, it would be sweeter, the sweetest thing he'd ever tasted. And it would have been so easy, so fucking easy—

But he hadn't. Like the fucking fool he still was, he'd pushed her away and told her they could only be friends.

Mac had done some shit in his lifetime that he wasn't proud of, shit that occasionally haunted his dreams even now, but pushing TR away that night at the wedding was his one big regret—even if it had been for her own good. She deserved so much more than what he could offer. Didn't she see that?

Apparently not, not if she was showing up nearly a year later and asking him to be her date.

But her date for *what?*

Mac drained the mug, barely noticing the burn of liquid as it slid down his throat. Nothing from this morning made sense—from TR showing up and dropping that whole date bombshell in his lap, to seeing that stupid fucking peashooter in her purse. Every instinct he possessed screamed that she was up to something. The question was: what?

Mac spun on his heel and bounded up the wooden steps. All it would take was one simple call and he should have his answer. Maybe—if he still had TR's number. If she'd answer. If she'd even tell him. The damn woman could be stubborn when she wanted to be.

Fair enough, because so could he.

chapter SIX

The dull throbbing at the base of her skull was growing stronger, strong enough that TR started digging through her tote bag for the bottle of ibuprofen as the crowded train pulled into Penn Station. Relief flooded her when her hand closed around the bottle. That, even more than the headache, was a huge sign that this afternoon had been a bigger failure than this morning.

Talk about shitty days.

She twisted the cap off and shook out three white tablets then immediately tossed them into her mouth. She capped the bottle, threw it back into her bag, then pulled out the bottle of water. Barely more than a sip remained but she didn't care—it was enough to wash the pills down. The way her head was pounding, she'd swallow them without the water.

All around her, busy commuters got to their feet, hands curled around briefcases or messenger bags tossed over shoulders. TR did the same, muttering an apology when she accidentally bumped into the man in front of her. He didn't even glance at her, just kept moving forward as the commuter train slowly emptied its passengers into the cold night.

Vapor lamps—dirty and dusty—pierced the darkness, throwing puddles of ineffectual light on the cracked concrete of the outside platform. More than half of the passengers were getting off at this main stop in Baltimore and TR was behind every single one of them, waiting as they made their way up the stairs.

She entered the warm air of the terminal and breathed a sigh of relief at being halfway home—until she thought of the long drive back to her place. It was rush hour, which meant I-83 would be backed up all the way to the beltway. With her luck, it would be at least another hour before she got home.

Well, the extended drive home would give her time to mull over this afternoon's meeting—such as it was. She still didn't understand how she'd lost control so quickly. It should have been an easy meeting, a quick interview about the training facility that would have given the Senator ample opportunity to expand on his greatness.

It had been anything but that.

She'd arrived fifteen minutes early, only to be told the Senator was running thirty minutes late. TR simply smiled and took a seat in an outer office, grateful that the overstuffed chair was plush and comfortable. She had other work with her—she always did—as well as reading material, so the delay didn't upset her. Then the half hour had turned into an hour. Frustrating, yes, but there was nothing she could do about it. She reworked some of the questions, already anticipating the possibility that the Senator might have to call the meeting short.

It was the meeting itself that still baffled her. The questions were basic, so basic that even a career politician shouldn't feel any need to put a spin on the answers.

The Senator had done a lot more than put spin on his answers, though. He hadn't even answered half the questions, instead repeating them back then going off on a tangent that had nothing to do with what she asked. He'd been distracted, at times looking at her as if he didn't remember her walking into his office. By the time she walked out, she was more confused than ever.

And more convinced there was something else going on.

What politician would pass up the opportunity to paint himself in a positive light? The answer: none. Only that was exactly what the Senator had done. It was like he'd been expecting negative blowback and had come out fighting without even listening to TR—not that most of what he said had even made sense.

The whole thing left her feeling...uneasy. Uncomfortable. Like she was being manipulated. Or misled. TR didn't like either feeling.

Maybe she just needed to distance herself for a few hours. Instead of mulling over the meeting during the long drive in traffic, she could listen to an audio book and get lost in a world of fiction for a little bit. Then, when she got home, she'd change into her comfy flannel pajama pants and her favorite thermal shirt, pour a glass of wine, and review her notes. She didn't record the interview—the Senator had been against that—but her notes were impeccable, jotted down almost verbatim in her own version of shorthand.

She stopped at the painfully small store near the exit of the train station for a fresh bottle of water, then detoured to the bathroom. That taken care of, she pushed through the old wooden doors leading outside, shivering as an icy blast of air blew over her. She stopped at the pay station before moving to the elevator to the parking garage and had just pushed the button when her phone started ringing from the recesses of her tote bag.

She was tempted to let the call go to voicemail then decided against it. It might be her editor, asking how the interview went. Or maybe it was her mom, calling to chat.

She didn't glance to see who the caller was, simply thumbed the screen to answer as the elevator doors opened and she stepped inside.

"Hello?"

There was a pause, long enough to make her think it was a robocall, or some telemarketer offering services she didn't need or want. TR almost hung up when the caller finally spoke; when he did, she nearly dropped the phone.

"What are you doing?"

"Um—" TR pulled the phone away from her ear and glanced at the screen, already knowing she'd see Mac's name. She frowned, pushed the button for the lower level of the garage, then lifted the phone back to her ear.

"I'm heading to my car. What are you doing?" And oh God, she sounded like she was a teenage girl talking to her crush for the first time—which was close enough to the truth that her face heated with embarrassment.

"You're just now leaving work?"

"No, I'm at Penn Station."

"What the hell are you doing down there?"

"I had to go to DC for an interview and decided to take the MARC down instead of driving."

"And you left from Penn Station? You couldn't have found a better place to catch the train?"

Why did he sound so angry? It was enough to set her teeth on edge and make the pounding at the base of her skull kick up a notch. "No, not when Penn Station is closer and more convenient."

"It's not exactly in the safest part of the city."

TR almost laughed—would have if her day had been even marginally better. But she didn't need to be lectured by the same man who was partially responsible for her crappy day and she didn't bother to hide her frustration when she spoke.

"There is nothing wrong with Penn Station." Mostly. "Thousands of people travel to and from Penn Station a week. More than thousands. I'll be fine."

"It's still not—"

"Is there a reason you called?" She cut him off, her voice a little sharper than she intended. Too bad. He was a big boy, he could handle it.

And that was probably the wrong thought to have. Mac *was* big—but he definitely wasn't a boy. The last thing she wanted—or needed—was images of his broad, hard body popping into her mind.

Yeah. Too late for that, because they were already there.

She muttered to herself then stepped off the elevator, readjusting the strap of her tote bag as she walked through the parking garage. The lights down here were dim, making the shadows deeper and longer.

Her heels clicked against the dirty concrete, the sound echoing in the cold night air as she moved deeper into the garage, toward the farthest row of parking spaces. It must be later than she realized because there weren't many cars left down here.

Of course, she had been one of the last passengers to leave the terminal, thanks to her stop for water and her trip to the bathroom. And probably thanks to Mac, too. She wouldn't have given the empty shadows a second thought if he hadn't opened his mouth—

"TR, are you still there?"

"Of course I'm still here. Where else would I be?"

"You sound a little...pissed off. Short."

She mentally rolled her eyes as she reached into her bag with her free hand, pulling out her keys. "It's been a really crappy day."

A short pause, filled with a grunt she could barely hear. "I guess that's my fault."

"Partly, yeah. But I'll get over it." TR finally reached her car then stumbled to a stop, a small sound of dismay falling from her mouth. She blinked, then blinked again, hoping she was only imagining things.

She wasn't.

The driver's side window was smashed, glass littering the front seat of her beloved little Camry. Both tires had been slashed and the driver's side door was dented and scratched near the door handle, like someone had tried to force it open before finally breaking the window. She took a hesitant step forward, stopped, then softly swore.

"You have got to be kidding me—"

"What's wrong?"

"I don't believe this. Dammit! After everything else today—"

"TR! What is it? What's going on?"

"I don't need this. I really don't. Dammit! Dammit—"

"TR. What the hell is going on? Talk to me. Now."

It was the command in Mac's rough voice that finally drew her attention away from her car. She blew out a sigh, the sound a heavy combination of sorrow and frustration, then ran a shaking hand through her hair.

"Somebody broke into my car."

"What?"

She ignored his low roar, tempted to do some roaring of her own. "Somebody broke into my car. The window's smashed and—"

"Get back upstairs. Now."

"I will. I want to take pictures first. Then I need to—"

"TR, listen to me. I want you to get back upstairs. Now. Don't take pictures. Don't do anything."

"But—"

"Is there anyone else there? Anyone around you?"

Dread washed over her, leaving icy tendrils of fear in its wake. She spun around, her eyes darting to the surrounding shadows, expecting someone to jump out at her. But she was the only person down here; the shadows were empty, hiding nothing more than discarded trash.

As far as she could tell.

She closed her eyes and took a deep breath, trying to calm her racing pulse even as she mentally cursed Mac for making her so nervous. Damn him. Even now, he was still talking, his voice low and rough, issuing commands she thought of ignoring simply on principle.

But she wasn't stupid and what Mac was telling her made sense. Any reasonable person would go straight upstairs and report it. There were police officers upstairs—Amtrak police and city police. Going upstairs was the smart thing to do.

"TR, did you hear me? Are you there?"

"Yes, I'm here." She gave her car one last long look, blinking against the unexpected tears, then turned and headed back to the elevator.

"Are you going upstairs?"

"Yes, I'm going upstairs."

"I'm coming to get you. Wait there for me—"

"You don't need to come get me. I can call for a ride—"

"I'm coming to get you."

"Mac, don't be ridiculous. It'll take you forever to get here with the traffic. I can—"

"Boomer's on his way. He'll be there in fifteen. Wait with him—"

"Who? What are you talking about? Mac, I don't need a babysitter. I'm going upstairs to report it now. Then I'll figure out how to get home after everything's been taken care of." TR pushed the *up* button, breathing a silent sigh of thanks when the doors opened right away. "I'll be fine—"

Mac kept talking as if he hadn't even heard her. Or maybe he had heard her and he was just ignoring her. Of course he was, because wasn't that what she needed to really put the cherry on top of this whole miserable day?

"Just wait with Boomer and don't do anything until I get there."

"Mac, I don't—"

"Please."

It was the *please* that made her stop. Not just the word, but the soft plea in Mac's gruff voice. TR blew out another sigh, all the fight leaving her with that one long breath. The day had been too long and filled with one miserable failure after another. She didn't have the desire to fight anything else, not right now. It would be a different story in the morning. It might even be different in an hour. But now...for now, it would just be easier to give in, to let Mac have his way. To let him take over and handle everything.

TR went back inside to wait.

chapter SEVEN

They were laughing.

He'd damn near broken his neck, fighting apprehension along with bumper-to-bumper traffic to get here, and they were both sitting there laughing.

Mac sucked in a deep breath and forced his hands to uncurl, when what he really wanted to do was wrap them around Boomer's thick neck and strangle the bastard. Son of a bitch. He pulled in another deep breath, forcing himself to calm down. What the fuck was wrong with him? Laughter was good. Laughter meant there was no immediate danger.

Hell, it probably meant there was no danger at all, period. Maybe he'd been overreacting. Maybe TR's car being broken into was nothing more than a random act. Shit like that happened all the time, it didn't have to mean she was targeted.

Except his gut was still clenched and those little fucking hairs on the back of his neck were still standing at attention. When that happened, he listened. It had saved his sorry ass on more than one occasion.

Had the break-in been nothing more than coincidence? Maybe.

But he wasn't buying it for a second. Not after this morning. Not with the way every instinct was screaming at him, telling him this was all connected to...he had no idea what. Whatever the hell TR was up to.

And she was up to something.

He watched her now, drinking in the sight of her sitting there on the old wooden bench that reminded him of a church pew with its high back and curved arms. Her long legs were crossed, her foot casually swaying mid-air. Not that impatient sway it had done this morning in his office, though. No, of course not. Not when she was sitting there, leaning toward Boomer, her full mouth curled into a relaxed smile. The other man leaned forward, his arm hovering near TR's shoulders, like he was about to slide her closer and pull her into a hug.

Or pull her onto his lap.

Mac would rip his fucking arm from its socket if he tried.

Boomer must have sensed the imminent danger because he leaned back, his dark gaze slowly sliding around the lobby before coming to a rest on Mac. He didn't move his arm, though, and that pissed Mac off.

He didn't bother to question why, he just strolled toward the pair, the soles of his sneakers squeaking against the polished tile floor. TR looked up, her smile dimming as frustration and something else flashed in those pale blue eyes. She uncrossed her legs and stood, her gaze narrowing the slightest bit as he approached.

"Good, you're finally here. That means I can leave now."

"Not yet. I want to take a look at the car first."

"You can't. They already had it towed to a body shop."

Mac shot a dangerous glare in Boomer's direction. "I told you to wait."

"Um, hello?" TR stepped toward him, waving a slim hand in his face. "It wasn't up to him, it was up to me."

"Actually, it wasn't her call. Amtrak police made arrangements for the tow not long after I got here. They didn't want it sitting around."

Mac swore under his breath. He knew they'd want to have it towed but he figured he'd have had time to go over it first. Then again, he hadn't figured it would take him this long to get down here. Hopefully Boomer had been able to take a look at it, get some pictures.

If he hadn't been totally distracted by TR, that is.

"Why do you even care if it was towed? Never mind, don't answer that. I don't care." TR grabbed a lightweight jacket that was entirely wrong for the cold weather from the bench and shrugged into it, then slung a large tote bag over her shoulder. "The only thing I care about it is getting home and having a nice glass of wine. Now that you're here, I can do that."

"Fine. I'll take you home."

TR shot him an incredulous look. "I don't need you to take me home. I can get my own ride."

"Why pay for a taxi when I'm offering?"

"Because—" Her mouth snapped shut and she narrowed her eyes. Mac could almost see her brain trying to figure out a good reason for turning him down. And he knew, just as she did, that there wasn't.

Not when they were heading in the same direction.

Unless she simply decided to tell him to go to hell because she was still pissed about this morning. There was a damn good chance she'd do exactly that.

Mac held his breath and waited, wondering what the hell he'd do if she did. TR must have decided it wasn't worth fighting him because she released a frustrated sigh and tossed her bag to the bench.

"Fine. Whatever. You can take me. Just let me use the restroom first."

Mac watched her walk away, pausing just long enough to enjoy the subtle sway of her hips before turning to Boomer. "Did you take a look around?"

"Yeah, just like you wanted me to."

"And?"

Boomer shrugged and rose to his feet. "Nothing jumped out. Looked like a random break-in."

Mac heard the doubt in the other man's voice. "Except?"

"Except they didn't steal anything. They tore through the glove box and under the seats. Hell, they even pulled up the floor mats. But the only thing taken was some loose change in a cup holder. At least, according to TR. No idea why anyone would go to all that trouble just for a couple of dollars in change."

"So you think it was random?"

Boomer frowned, his eyes going carefully blank as he looked inward, no doubt reviewing every little detail he'd seen. That was one of Boomer's many talents—a photographic memory combined with an uncanny ability to put things together, even when half of the puzzle pieces were missing. A few seconds passed before the man's gaze shot back to Mac.

"On the surface, it looks random, like maybe a

couple kids were up to no good. Her car was parked far enough away that being seen wouldn't be an issue, and the security cameras were conveniently not working."

"But?"

"If that was it, why was it just her car that was broken into? Usually, in a case like this, you'd have a few cars being hit. My gut says something else is going on."

"Mine too. Did you get pictures?"

"Yeah." Boomer patted the phone clipped to his waist. "Not that I think they'll show anything. I'll get them sent over to you."

"Thanks." Mac glanced over his shoulder then turned back. "You can get lost now."

"Why did I have a feeling you were going to say that?"

Mac folded his arms in front of him and leveled the other man with a dark glare. "Because you have a finely-honed instinct for self-preservation?"

Boomer laughed then clapped him on the shoulder. "You think? Yeah, I figured there was more going on there. By the way, you owe me. Big time."

"For coming down here? Fine, if you say so."

"No, not for that. Well, not just that."

"Then for what?"

"For turning your girl down when she asked me out for New Year's Eve."

The blood froze in Mac's veins for a long second, then quickly melted under the heat of his unexpected rage. His voice was deathly quiet when he spoke. "Excuse me?"

"Calm down, He-Man. I told you—I turned her down. Apparently just like you did." Boomer stepped forward and lowered his voice. "But if you don't change your mind, I think I might take her up on her offer."

"Only if you want me to snap your neck like a twig."

"Zeus might get a little pissed at you taking out one of the team like that."

"Fuck Daryl. He'll get over it. But you won't if you even think about—"

"Then get your head out of your ass and tell her you changed your mind."

"It's not that simple—"

"The hell it ain't." Boomer stepped back then lifted his hand in a quick wave—not at Mac, but at someone behind him. He turned and saw TR a few feet away, her brows lowered in a frown as she watched them.

How long had she been standing there? Had she heard anything they'd said? Mac turned back to Boomer to ask but the other man was already walking away.

"What was that all about?"

"Nothing."

TR's brows shot upward in disbelief but she didn't push—maybe because she realized it would be an exercise in futility. She made a small humming sound then scooped up her tote bag. "If you say so. Are you ready?"

"Whenever you are." He swept his arm out, motioning her to lead the way, then fell into step behind her.

Ready? Hell no. When it came to TR, he'd never be ready.

chapter
EIGHT

The oversized tires hugged the wet asphalt, the constant humming sound muted from the interior of the truck. Traffic was still heavy, the red glow of taillights snaking in front of them as far as Mac could see. Rush hour should have been over by now—would have been, if not for the arrival of the cold rain. If the temperature continued dropping, the wet roads would turn icy and create an even bigger driving headache.

Mac planned on having TR home before that happened.

He glanced over at her, watching as the streetlights along the side of the highway cast her profile in alternating pools of light and shadow. She'd been quiet ever since they'd left Penn Station, her gaze focused on something ahead of them that he couldn't see. Her mouth was pressed tight and tension radiated from every line of her stiff body. Anger? Maybe. At him? Probably.

But something told him there was more to it than that. What he saw—what he *felt*—was more than anger. There was an aura of frustration and disappointment surrounding her, thick enough that he wanted to reach over and pull her into a hug and tell her everything would be okay.

Yeah. Because pulling TR across the truck's console and into his lap would really help things.

He tightened his grip on the steering wheel and studied the traffic around him, watching for drivers trying to merge to the right. This section of the inner loop, where I-83 and 695 ran next to each other, could be treacherous at the best of times. Add in the fact that it was dark *and* raining, and you had a recipe for a collision just waiting to happen.

No sooner had he had that thought than the car next to him tried to whip over into his lane. Mac tapped the breaks, swearing softly as horns blared around him. The car zoomed in front of him then immediately hit its breaks to avoid ass-ending the car in front of him. Mac slowed even more, muttering briefly to himself before once again glancing at his passenger.

TR hadn't moved, not even to grip the panic bar above the door. There was no indication she had even noticed the near-miss; if she had, Mac was certain she would have said something.

But there was only silence.

"You're awfully quiet."

She turned her head toward him, her gaze barely meeting his, then went back to staring straight ahead. "I have a headache."

His hand moved to the center console, ready to open it. "I've got some aspirin—"

"I took some earlier. When I was getting off the

train."

"And that was nearly three hours ago. Are you sure—"

"Yeah."

Mac moved his hand away from the console, let it hover between them for a brief second before grabbing the steering wheel once more. "You never said why you went to DC."

"An interview. I told you that."

Had she? Yes, she had—right before sending him into the small freak-out when she said her car had been broken into. "What was the interview for? A new story? Something else?"

"A story. Nothing exciting."

There was something in her voice that made him frown and look over. She'd been too bland when she answered, too *controlled*. "Why don't you tell me about it?"

A pause, followed by the smallest shift as her body stiffened. "Nothing to tell. It's just a story."

"You don't sound very enthusiastic about it."

"Mac, can you do me a favor and just let it go? It's been a really long, really crappy day. I have a headache. I'm tired. My car is trashed. All I want to do is get home, change out of these clothes, have a glass of wine, and go to sleep. Okay?"

"Yeah. Sure." He nodded and turned his attention back to the traffic. The flow sped up for a few minutes then slowed back to an agonizing crawl as vehicles maneuvered the sharp curve to northbound I-83. Traffic stopped, lurched forward, then stopped again as cars tried to push their way into the far-right lane to exit onto Timonium Road.

"I, um—" He stopped, cleared his throat, started

again. "I'm sorry."

TR sighed then darted a quick glance in his direction. "For what?"

"For, you know, getting your day off to a crappy start."

"I never said—"

"Not in so many words, no." He risked another glance in her direction. "But the inference was there. And I'm sorry."

"Fine. Apology accepted."

"Wow. Let me mark this day in my calendar. TR Meyers accepted my apology without a shit-ton of grief." Mac glanced over, caught the briefest of smiles curl her mouth before she hid it with her hand. A second later, that same hand shot out and playfully smacked him on the arm.

"You're still a smartass, I see."

Mac grunted, the sound part laughter, part disbelief. "You'd be the only one to think so."

"Why don't I believe that?"

Because you're the only one who sees this part of me. Mac didn't say the words out loud. They sounded too cynical, too bitter. And TR wouldn't believe him, anyway, even if it was true. Yeah, Daryl and Jon saw this side of him, but that was it. There were very few people he felt comfortable enough with to let his guard down—less than he could count on one hand. TR happened to be one of those people.

She just didn't know it.

Traffic was moving a little faster now as they approached the Warren Road exit. He glanced in the sideview mirror then eased his way to the right lane just as TR started to point.

"This is the exit—"

"I know."

Two little words. They shouldn't have meant anything but from the expression on TR's face, you'd think he had just told her that Santa Claus was real. She watched him with stunned eyes, her mouth slightly ajar.

"How do you know where I live?"

"I've been there before, remember?"

"Yeah, but that was over a year ago. For all you know, I could have moved."

"Did you?"

"No, but—"

"Then what's the problem?"

"You've only been there once. How do you remember?"

"I just do. Christ, TR, it's not that big a deal." Were the words too rough? Was his voice a little too gruff? Maybe. But he didn't want her to make a big deal out of it, didn't want her to get the wrong impression. So he remembered where she lived. Big deal.

He thought she was going to say something else—it sure as hell looked like she wanted to. But she simply shook her head then leaned back in the leather seat, some of the tension he had noticed earlier leaving her.

Neither one of them said anything else as he maneuvered the big truck along Warren Road, crossing over York Road and heading east to Bosley. Ten minutes later, he was pulling into the apartment complex where she lived, slowing down as he searched for a parking space.

"You can just drop me off—"

"I'll walk you in."

She wanted to argue with him, he knew it just from that look in her eye. To his surprise, she kept quiet—although her expression let him know exactly what she thought of his suggestion. Well, she'd just have to get over it. He would have walked her in regardless—he'd done that the last time he had dropped her off, over a year ago. No way in hell would he let her go in by herself now, not after what had happened to her car.

Not when those little hairs on the back of his neck were still standing at attention.

He circled the parking lot twice, swearing under his breath at the lack of spaces. He finally made his own space along a grassy break and parallel parked near the curb not far from the hydrant. Yes, he was taking a chance of getting a ticket—but he wasn't going to be here that long, and he doubted there were many police officers driving around the numerous apartment complexes looking for parking violations.

He opened the door and jumped out then quickly moved around the side to help TR. But she was already lowering herself to the ground, one hand wrapped around the inside door handle for balance. He took the tote bag from her and slung it over his shoulder then offered his arm. She hesitated then finally accepted it, holding onto him for support as she stepped off the running board. She moved her hand as soon as her feet touched the ground then motioned to her tote bag.

"My keys are in my bag."

Mac handed her the bag, listening as she rooted around the depths for her keys. He glanced around the lot, his gaze taking in the parked cars and the deep shadows between them. Watching. Studying. Searching.

He saw only shadows. Not just between the cars, but along the walkways to the adjoining buildings and even around the buildings themselves. The complex was an older one, established and well-maintained with large trees and mature bushes—and plenty of spaces for someone to hide.

"You really don't need to walk me in. I'm a big girl. I can take care of myself."

Mac followed her up the sidewalk then moved in front of her to open the door. "Never said you couldn't."

TR muttered something under her breath. The words were indistinct but the tone wasn't. Mac didn't bother to ask her to repeat herself, not when he knew she was grumbling about him.

TR lived in the last building of the complex, the one that backed up to a small patch of wooded land. Each building had three floors, with four apartments on each floor. And she, of course, lived on the bottom floor, in the apartment in the back corner. He had commented about it the last time he'd been here—the night of Jonathan's wedding. But she had simply shrugged off his security concerns, telling him she liked the sense of privacy, along with the ability to simply walk outside to her patio and enjoy the quiet allure of nature.

He followed her down the steps, thinking of that night nearly a year ago. If he'd accepted her quiet invitation, would they be together now? Or would it have been nothing more than a fling, over before it really started? Would she have grown tired of the horrified stares and harsh whispers and pitying glances that accompanied him everywhere he went? Would she have grown frustrated with his silent tendencies or the sudden absences required by his job?

Maybe. Maybe not. It didn't matter. Not now, not after all this time. Not when he knew nothing had changed since that night. There could be nothing between them except friendship, not even now.

Chapter NINE

TR was completely unaware of his thoughts, his regrets. And that was the way it needed to be. If she ever found out, ever got just an inkling—no, he couldn't allow that to happen. She was the one person who had the uncanny ability to knock him off-balance and keep him that way. If she ever found out, she'd be relentless in tearing down his walls.

So Mac kept his mouth shut and his thoughts—and regrets—to himself as TR unlocked the door to her apartment. She pushed it open, reaching out with her free hand to skim the light switch to the left. Soft light filled the entranceway, which was nothing more than a small extension of the living room, separated by a few square feet of tile instead of carpet.

Mac entered behind her then stood just inside, his gaze scanning the living room. An overstuffed loveseat was pushed against the wall, throw pillows adding a bright splash of color to the neutral upholstery. A matching chair, also overstuffed, was placed perpendicular to the loveseat. The furniture was the same but the area rug—a large rectangle of blues and greens—was new. So was the small Christmas tree placed on an accent table near the patio doors.

TR dropped her bag to the chair and tossed the keys to the coffee table with one smooth motion. She moved over to the small tree and leaned down, thumbing the built-in switch until clear white lights twinkled on the plastic branches. Then she straightened and turned, eyeing him with a wariness that caught him off-guard.

"Okay. I'm safe inside. You can go now."

Mac closed the door behind him, ignored her surprise. "Not until I look around."

"Mac, there's nobody here." She spread her arms wide, encompassing the living room and dining room, the small kitchen, the short hallway. "It isn't that big."

"Still plenty of places to hide. Closets. The bedroom. The bathroom—"

"No. No, you don't get to do this."

"What am I doing?"

"Making me paranoid in my own home. I'm safe here. Nobody's hiding. Nobody's coming after me. Nobody's going to jump out at me."

"Never said there was." He stepped further into the living room, frowning when he noticed the safety bar for the sliding glass door was unlatched. He moved over and slid it into place then checked to make sure the door was locked.

"You should keep the safety bar in place."

"I do. Every night before I go to bed."

He gave her a look that let her know what he thought of that then moved down the hallway, stopping to study the small kitchen before moving to the bathroom. TR muttered something under her breath as he pulled back the shower curtain.

"Do you plan on checking under my bed, too? Because I have to tell you, there's probably a killer dust bunny waiting there, ready to gobble you up."

Mac allowed himself a small smile at her sarcasm then quickly schooled his face before turning back to her. "Now who's the smartass?"

"I wasn't being a smartass. I told you, I'm just tired." She spun on her heel, heading toward her bedroom. Mac followed, hesitating for only a second when he caught sight of the bed in the middle of the room.

Yeah, because seeing a bed in a *bedroom* was such an unusual thing.

He gave himself a mental shake and forced his gaze away from the rumpled comforter. Told himself to pay no attention to the pale green sheets or the fluffy pillows—

Or to the colorful scraps of lace tossed on the dresser against the wall.

TR must have noticed them at the same time because she rushed over and snagged the bra and matching thong then quickly tossed them into the small hamper. A flush of pink stained her cheeks as she shot a cautious glance in his direction.

"I, uh, I was running late this morning. I'm usually not this sloppy."

"I'm not grading you on your housekeeping skills."

"Oh, goody. Just what are you grading me on? Never mind, I don't want to know." She started past him, her arm brushing against his chest as she moved toward the hallway. "C'mon, Mac. Out. You've scared off all the boogeymen, now it's time for you to leave so I can get some sleep."

"I thought you were going to have that glass of wine first."

TR stopped in the hallway, sighing loudly before shooting him an impatient look over her shoulder. Another sigh, then she continued on to the kitchen. "I am. As soon as you leave."

Mac propped his shoulder against the doorway separating the kitchen from the dining area and simply watched her as she opened a cabinet and pulled down a stemless wine glass. She ignored him as she reached into the refrigerator and grabbed an almost-full bottle of white wine from the top shelf.

"Just one glass?" His voice held the faintest hint of teasing. The question earned him an impatient frown.

"Since when do you drink wine?"

He didn't, not usually. Bourbon was generally his choice of drink but he knew she didn't have any on hand. But he didn't say any of that, just simply shrugged. "Nothing wrong with an occasional glass of wine."

TR snorted, the sound somehow oddly feminine even as it conveyed both her disbelief and impatience. She poured wine into her glass, corked the bottle, then turned to lean against the counter. Her clear gaze caught his for a few long seconds then slid away.

"Not going to offer me any, huh?"

"How about you tell me what you really want first?"

"Who says I want anything?" And Christ, what a fucking lie that was. What he wanted was *her*—he had from damn near the first time he'd seen her. Not that it made any difference. He couldn't act on that desire now any more than he could a year ago.

Could TR tell what he was thinking? Christ, he hoped to fuck not. No, she couldn't, he was positive of it. She was too preoccupied with whatever else was going on to pay any attention to what he was thinking.

She blew out a tired sigh then raised the glass to her mouth and took a long sip. Only after that did her gaze return to his. Frustration and impatience were reflected in her pale blue eyes, along with apprehension and worry. Her eyes grew a little brighter and the overhead light reflected off the film of moisture that appeared in their depths. Mac's gut clenched when he realized she was going to start crying. And fuck, what the hell was he supposed to do now? He could handle damn near anything thrown his way—bullets, blood, pain. But the sight of those tears growing in TR's eyes? Fuck no. He had no idea what to do. If she started crying—

TR blinked and the tears were gone, replaced by a weariness that made him want to step forward and wrap her in his arms and tell her everything would be okay. Mac curled his hands into fists and shoved them in the back pockets of his jeans, afraid he'd do just that.

He couldn't, no matter how much he might want to.

"Tell me more about this party you invited me to this morning."

TR's head snapped up, surprise flashing in her eyes. She took another sip of wine, this one a little longer. "It's just a New Year's Eve party. A black-tie affair down in DC."

"So I need a tux?"

Her gaze snapped to his. "*You* don't need

anything. I found someone else to go with me."

"Is that a fact?"

"Yeah. Ryder's taking me."

"Who?" Mac frowned, his mind going blank for a frantic second before the name clicked. Ryder. Ryder Hess. *Boomer.*

"You know: Ryder. The guy you sent to babysit me a few hours ago?"

Mac chuckled, the sound rough and edgy and maybe even a little rusty. "He wasn't babysitting, he was keeping an eye on you until I got there—"

"Which pretty much defines *babysitting*—"

"—and Boomer isn't taking you anywhere."

"Yeah, he is. He said—"

"He turned you down."

"He might change his mind."

"He won't. And he's not taking you. *I* am."

"I don't want—"

"You asked me. I answered."

"Yeah, and that answer was *no*. A very vehement *no*. You were extremely clear—"

"I changed my mind."

TR looked like she was ready to dig her heels in and start arguing. Not that Mac could blame her; he wouldn't expect anything else from her, especially after the evening she'd had. But she surprised him by carelessly shrugging her shoulders, like it didn't make any difference to her at all.

"Fine. Whatever."

"That's it? No argument?"

"I'm too tired to argue."

Mac watched her for a long minute, noticed the strain around her full mouth, the exhaustion in her eyes. Not just exhaustion, but worry as well. He straightened away from the doorjamb and stepped toward her. Stopped. Took a step back and swallowed back a silent growl.

"You going to tell me what's going on?"

"Nothing's going on."

"You know you can talk to me, right?"

"Mac, there's nothing to talk about. I'm just—" She hesitated for a few seconds, frowning as she stared into the wine glass cupped between her hands. "I'm just working out some different angles on this story and it's giving me fits, that's all."

Did he believe her? For the most part, yes. But there was something else going on, something she wasn't telling him. He didn't think she was being deliberately evasive, though.

Should he push? Ask for more details? No, not tonight. He could see the exhaustion on her face, feel the frustration rolling off her. Pushing her would only make her more frustrated—and probably a little angry, as well.

"Maybe sleeping on it will help."

Was that relief he saw flash in her eyes? "Yeah. Maybe."

"Then I'll let you get to sleep." Mac stepped out of the kitchen, waited for her to follow him to the door. "Lock the door behind me."

"I plan on it."

He nodded and opened the door then paused, one hand still on the knob. "Come by tomorrow and I'll take you to the range. Show you how to use that peashooter of yours."

Surprise flashed in her eyes a second before they narrowed in suspicion. "Why?"

"Why not?"

"Just like that? You're going to take me shooting then give the gun back?"

"Only if I'm comfortable with you having it back."

"Fine."

"And only after you tell me what's going on."

"I told you, nothing is going on."

Mac watched her for a long second then stepped toward her, so close their bodies nearly touched. Surprise flared in her eyes and she reached up, placed one hand in the center of his chest. It was the touch of her hand, the slight trembling of her slender fingers, that made him stop and realize what he'd been about to do.

She didn't push him away—no, she wasn't smart enough to do that, wasn't smart enough to step back and tell him to get lost. And dammit, he could see the need in her gaze, in the way her mouth parted ever so slightly as her tongue darted out and swiped along her lower lip. All he wanted was one taste, one taste to carry him through his lonely nights—

Fuck.

What was he doing? Why had he moved so close to her? He needed to step back, put distance between them before he did something they'd both regret.

No. Something *she'd* regret. And she would. Maybe not tonight, maybe not tomorrow—but eventually, and sooner rather than later.

As soon as she realized he wasn't a shining knight but rather a tarnished, jaded rogue.

Mac took a steadying breath then stepped back, ignoring the disappointment welling in her gaze as her hand dropped to her side. It was that disappointment that made him lean forward once more and press a quick kiss against her forehead. He didn't wait for her response, simply stepped into the hallway and glanced at a spot over her shoulder.

"We'll talk more tomorrow."

She nodded then quickly shut the door. Only after he heard the click of the deadbolt being turned did Mac breathe a sigh of relief and turn toward the stairs.

And wonder what the fuck he'd just done. He should have never touched her, not even for that innocent kiss. Because now he wanted more of her, more than ever before—

And he knew that could never happen.

chapter TEN

The man sat in the car and watched. He was in no danger of being seen—the car blended in with all the vehicles parked around the complex. The windows were tinted, hiding his silhouette. The rain made things challenging but cracking them two inches prevented condensation from forming. It also stopped people from hesitating and looking around. People were always so afraid of rain, afraid to get wet, afraid to take their time—or take notice of their surroundings.

But the rain—and the dark of night—were his companions. His assistants.

Comforting him. Hiding him.

The man who had accompanied the woman into her apartment was a surprise. He was unknown and, therefore, suspicious. Large. Broad. Muscular. One look had convinced him the man was former military. Possibly a police officer.

No, not a police officer. There was something too

sharp and controlled about his movements, too stealthy, too *aware*. Military then. Maybe Special Forces. Maybe Black Ops.

And didn't that make things interesting?

No matter. He was always up for a challenge. He simply committed the truck's tag number to memory and sat back to watch. To wait.

Was the man an acquaintance? A friend? Something more? There had been no information about a boyfriend but information was only as reliable as its source—and sometimes, not even then. And his source—his client—was less reliable than he'd prefer.

Panic did that to people. Made them act before thinking. Made them take steps they wouldn't normally take if they stopped to consider the ramifications first. That was why his client found himself in such an untenable situation.

More untenable than he realized.

But the man was paid—paid very well, indeed—to act, not advise, so he would wait and watch and rely on his instinct instead of the haphazard information he'd been given.

The door of the apartment building opened and the man who had entered twenty minutes earlier walked out. He paused on the sidewalk, the frown on his scarred face visible even from this distance. He glanced around, his frown deepening for a few seconds before he shook his head then returned to his truck and climbed in.

Breath held, his body as still as a day-old corpse, the man watching didn't move. A few minutes later, the truck was gone and the man was left alone again, a nefarious sentinel hidden by night and shadow.

Should he go back inside the apartment and

continue his search? No. As tempting as the challenge might be—to search while the woman slept, unaware—there was no need. He'd seen enough in the time he had already searched.

What he was looking for wasn't there, just as it hadn't been in her car.

Just as he had known it wouldn't be.

Vandalizing the car had been unnecessary but his client had insisted, certain that it would delay the woman's return to her apartment. The man had considered talking his client out of it then decided against it. His client liked being in control—even if that control was nothing more than an illusion.

A faint vibration came from his pocket, the movement lasting no more than a second. He pulled the phone out, not bothering to glance at the blacked-out screen. Only one person had this number and he had been expecting the call.

"Yes." His voice was quiet, well-modulated, giving away nothing that could be used to later describe him.

Unlike the caller's voice, which was filled with impatience and irritation and—under that—a tell-tale strain. "I expected a report by now. Do you have what I sent you for?"

"No. It wasn't in either her car or her apartment."

"Dammit. I need that information. Now. I need to find out what she knows."

If the man had a sense of humor, he might have chuckled at his client's frustration. He might have even told his client that his expectations were unrealistic, that he was jumping to dangerous conclusions. But his emotions had been leeched from him through years of training, leaving him with nothing but a tightly-reined control.

And it wasn't his place to share his opinions with the clients.

The man stared straight ahead, his voice carefully neutral as he spoke. "I believe that she carries any information she might have with her."

If she had any information—which he suspected she didn't. But his client was too impatient, too frightened, to consider that possibility. The muttered string of profanity was a clear indication of that.

"Dammit, I'm not paying you for your opinion. I need that information. Now. I need to find out what she knows."

Did the client realize he had repeated himself? The occurrences were happening more frequently, something the man had noticed the last few weeks. He had become a liability, even though he hadn't yet realized it.

"I can look again tonight while she's sleeping. Take care of her as well."

"No, that's too risky. It might raise suspicion if something were to happen to her after this evening's incident." There was a sharp sigh, followed by a long pause of silence.

The man imagined his client sitting back in his expensive leather chair, his manicured fingers pinching the bridge of his nose. He had never met his client in person, wasn't supposed to know who he was.

But he did. The man had made it a point to know. Had studied him, knew his strengths and weaknesses, knew he had many more of the latter and very few of the former.

"We need to let things quiet down for a few days. Stand down for now. We can resume our plans at the party. That would probably be a better time to get to her, anyway. I'll be in touch with you before then."

The party would be the worst time but the man kept his opinion to himself. "Of course, sir." The words spilled into silence, heard only by himself since the call had already been disconnected.

That was fine with him. Let the client think he was in charge, let him think he was the one making the decisions.

The man knew better.

He carefully placed the phone back into his pocket, knowing he would dispose of it later tonight. Then he focused his gaze on the building in front of him.

Thinking. Planning. Relishing the feel of his hands around a slender throat, watching flesh bruise and eyes bulge as the last breath of life escaped the woman's body.

Imagining the thrust of a blade sliding between his client's ribs, sinking deep into flesh and muscle. Feeling the hot wash of blood rushing over his hands as he twisted the knife, dragging out the moment of death.

The woman first, then the client.

He did, after all, have his orders.

chapter ELEVEN

"What do you know about the Senate Committee on Armed Services?"

TR would have been disappointed if she expected the question to distract Mac because he didn't even pause before sighting in his target and firing. One shot, then another and another, the sound muted by the hearing protectors she wore. No, he wasn't distracted at all. In fact, he didn't give any indication he had even heard her.

And maybe he hadn't. Maybe her voice had been too low for him to hear through his own hearing protectors.

He ejected the clip, checked to make sure the barrel was empty, then carefully placed the gun—the *pistol*—on the wooden platform in front of him. He tugged the padded protectors down around his neck then turned to look at her.

"What do you want to know?"

So he *had* heard her.

She shrugged, carefully avoiding his gaze. "I don't know. Just general stuff, I guess."

"They have legislative oversight of the military, including the DoD. Military R&D—research and development. Oversight on nuclear energy pertaining to national security" Mac's lips curled into something that wasn't quite a smile. "And my personal favorite: military benefits."

"Yeah, I read all that online, too. I want to know what you *can't* find online."

"You said you were looking for general stuff."

"Okay, maybe more than just general stuff."

Mac watched her for a long minute, his dark gaze so intent that she looked away. That didn't stop her skin from prickling, didn't stop her heart from skipping. Didn't stop the heat of awareness from washing over her.

And damn him for making her feel that way. Again. Who was she kidding? She had never stopped feeling that way—excited, needy, anxious. Sweaty palms. Knotted stomach. Racing pulse. All of it. She had been so sure she'd gotten over it this past year—right up until seeing him again yesterday morning.

Right up until that gentle kiss last night.

If you could even call that a kiss. It had been more like a peck, more of a—

She pulled her thoughts away from that whole line of thinking. That way lie madness...and she was already dealing with enough madness, seeing hidden agendas and cover-ups where none existed. She didn't need to add to it.

Mac finally pulled his gaze from her, giving her time to catch her breath. "Does this have anything to do with that story you're working on that you won't tell me about?"

"No. At least, I don't think so."

He folded his arms across his broad chest. The sleeves of his black t-shirt pulled tight around his biceps and she briefly wondered how many shirts he stretched out every week simply by wearing them.

Then she realized where those thoughts were leading and quickly looked away, focusing her gaze on the emblem printed on his shirt. It was an elongated skull in white, with *C.S.S.* in block letters underneath. *Cover Six Security*, the name of the company he ran with Daryl Anderson and Jonathan Reigler.

She pointed to it with a questioning glance. "What does that mean, anyway? *Cover Six*?"

"Covering your six. Your back. If someone's covering your six, it means they've got your back. They're watching out for you."

"I didn't know that." TR forced a smile and nodded, like he'd been waiting for her approval all along. "I like it. Think I can get a shirt?"

Mac blinked, the barest hint of disbelief flashing in his eyes. Had she finally surprised him? Yes, she had. TR would have done a little happy dance if his surprise hadn't been so quickly followed by a growling frown.

"Think you can maybe stop changing the subject?"

"I wasn't changing—" She stopped midsentence and looked away with a sigh. Olay, maybe she was. Not deliberately, though. She simply didn't know how to answer, not without sounding delusional.

"Why are you asking about the SASC?"

"The what?"

"The Committee on Armed Services."

"No real reason." She held up her hands, waving

off whatever he'd been about to say. "Honest. I'm just doing a story on the construction of a new training facility, that's it."

"The one outside Frederick?"

"Yeah. How'd you know about it?"

"Not exactly like it's top secret information."

"Oh." It was silly to be disappointed, silly to think that maybe Mac had some inside information she could use. But inside information about *what*? That's what she couldn't figure out.

Should she tell him about that cryptic email? Tell him about yesterday's odd interview with the Senator? No and no. He'd think she was losing her mind. Or worse than that, he'd figure out the real reason she needed him to go to the party with her was to provide cover so she could snoop around.

Somehow, she couldn't see Mac going along with that, so it was better not to say anything and simply change the subject.

"So. Can I have my gun back?"

"No." He turned his back on her and started cleaning up.

"Why not? I wasn't that bad."

"With the .25, no. But you need more practice with everything else."

"But I don't want anything else. I like my gun."

"The only thing that tiny thing would do is piss off whoever was coming after you, and that was if you managed to hit them. You'd have better luck just throwing the damn thing at their head."

"Hey, that's not very nice."

"It's the truth." Mac finished collecting the spent brass and placed them in a metal container, then locked both pistols in a black padded box. "If you're serious about learning how to use a weapon, then I'll teach you. We'll fire different types, find one you're comfortable with that's also effective."

"You'd really do that for me?"

"Yeah, I would—if you're serious."

"I am."

"Then we'll schedule more range time after the first of the year. At least twice a week, as long as I'm here. And if I'm not, I'll get one of the other guys to stand in for me if they're available."

TR nodded, momentarily stunned speechless. That he would offer to do that for her—

Probably meant nothing. She had to stop reading into every little thing Mac said or did. It hadn't helped a year ago, and it wasn't going to help now.

TR glanced at her watch then grabbed her coat from the bench behind her. "Thanks, Mac. I mean it."

"Yeah, no problem."

"I, uh, I have to go. I have a meeting in an hour. About tomorrow night—"

"I know: black tie. Meet at our office at nineteen-hundred-hours. Seven pm." He looked up, a scowl twisting the scars on the lower half of his face. "I still don't understand why you want to meet me there when I could just pick you up."

"Because I don't want you to have to drive out of your way."

"It's not out of my way—"

"I have to go." She cut him off before he could argue again. Then, on an impulse she didn't understand and didn't stop to question, she leaned up on her toes and placed a quick kiss against his cheek. "Thanks, Mac. I owe you one."

She turned away just in time to hide her smile,

knowing that he was staring at her in open-mouthed shock. She hadn't missed the way his body had stiffened in surprise, hadn't missed the sharp inhale of his breath when her lips brushed against his rough jaw.

And she hadn't missed the furious color that had flooded his face before she turned away.

The party tomorrow night was supposed to be for work only, a chance to snoop around and learn something. Or even make a few new contacts she could use in the future. But maybe, with just a little luck, it wouldn't be all about the job.

chapter TWELVE

Nerves ran roughshod over her entire body. The fluttery apprehension wasn't a feeling she was accustomed to and a small part of her wanted to laugh. The only reason she didn't was the fear she wouldn't stop once she started.

It was ridiculous to be nervous. This was business, not a *date*. That didn't stop the tiny hope flickering somewhere deep inside her, though. No matter how many times she tried to quash it, it refused to go away.

Fine. She'd simply have to ignore it.

She pulled in a deep breath, wincing when the nipped waist of the gown pulled tight. She glanced down then swallowed back a groan at the expanse of pale flesh that greeted her gaze.

Why, oh *why*, had she thought this gown was perfect?

Because it looked amazing when she had tried it on, that was why. It was a simple black gown, the cut classic and elegant, the material holding just a bit of shimmer. The bodice crisscrossed in the center, the material twisting into a strap that tied behind her neck. The back was open, forming a V at her lower back before falling in gentle folds around her hips and legs. The only adornment was a simple brooch of sparkling crystals pinned where the material gathered in the center of the bodice—right between her breasts.

The gown wasn't low-cut, not by any stretch of the imagination. But her flesh was still exposed, from her cleavage up—something else she wasn't accustomed to. She had a matching wrap which she could use to cover herself, which eased that worry just a bit.

But there were other worries as well. How would the gown compare to others who'd be at the party? Would the sparkling crystals appear tacky among the glittering jewels that would surely be on display? Did her gown—which cost nearly an entire week's paycheck—scream discount knock-off?

And could she possibly do anything else to procrastinate getting out of the rental car and going inside to meet Mac?

Yes, she could—but only as long as it took to check her hair and make-up in the visor mirror. Once that was done, she sucked in another breath—not quite as deep as the first one—and forced herself to get out of the car.

Cold air bit into her exposed flesh, causing her to shiver. She again questioned her choice of gown, but for more practical reasons this time: it did nothing to protect her against the below-freezing temperatures or the fine pellets of icy snow that had started to fall an hour ago.

She adjusted the wrap around her bare shoulders

and cautiously made her way to the door. The ground wasn't slick—at least, not yet—but she didn't need to lose her footing, not in the four-inch heels she was wearing.

The heavy door opened before she could reach it and she stumbled, nearly fell before catching herself. The cold air cloaking her disappeared, pushed back by a burning warmth that started in her center and quickly spread.

She had only seen Mac dressed up once, when he wore a suit at Jonathan and Sammie's wedding almost a year ago. The sight had stunned her, filled her with a feminine appreciation that she tried to keep hidden. In a misguided effort to disguise her reaction, she had teased him about cleaning up well.

She had never been more wrong.

The image of Mac in a suit was a balm to any woman's eyes. But Mac in a tux? He was...breathtaking. An image of pure masculine beauty that would make any woman sit up and take notice—and immediately wonder what she could do to take him home.

Did he have any idea of the image he presented? Raw. Untamed. Powerful. Pure male, in the most basic sense of the word. No, he didn't know. Not Mac. Humble, quiet, reserved. Self-conscious. Convinced his scars made him some kind of monster, convinced that people only saw those physical imperfections instead of the man he really was.

God help womankind if he ever realized the truth.

God help *her* if he ever realized the truth.

How long did she stand there, simply staring at him? Long enough for Mac to appear at her side before she'd had a chance to realize he had even moved. He had an open umbrella in one hand and he positioned it to protect her from the falling pellets. She tilted her head back and met his gaze, knew she should say something or do something, but her mind couldn't focus enough to find any words. There were no words adequate enough to capture her thoughts, to describe her visceral reaction to him.

Mac was the one who finally spoke, his voice low and rough as he stared down at her. "You're beautiful."

"I..." Her voice faded. There was nothing else she could say. The words faded before she could even find them, her mind still whirling—not at the image Mac presented, not this time. It was the way he looked at her, appreciation warming his dark eyes, warming *her*.

And oh God, she was in trouble. So much trouble. How could she have made such a huge mistake? She had invited Mac tonight to serve as a distraction so she could snoop around if she had the chance. They hadn't even left yet and the plan had already failed miserably.

Yes, Mac was a distraction—for her. For her state of mind, for her well-being, for her safety.

Mac placed one callused hand in the middle of her back, gently easing her forward. "You're also going to freeze to death if we stay outside."

"I—" Oh God, what was with her that she couldn't even talk? It was too much, the sight of Mac in a tux that accented his broad shoulders and wide chest, his lean hips and powerful legs; the feel of Mac's rough hand, so gentle and warm against the bare flesh of her back. Her senses were overloaded, her mind struggling to make sense of it all.

It was the sight of Mac's truck, as large and looming as the man himself, that finally kicked her mind into gear. She hesitated on the walkway and shook her head. "We should take my car. I don't think

I'll be able to climb up in that—"

"Already taken care of." Mac kept walking, guiding her around the back of the truck. A shiny black Mercedes S-Class sat next to it, the engine already running. He opened the passenger door then bent forward in a slight bow, one corner of his mouth curled up in a crooked grin. "Madam, your chariot awaits."

The bubbling laughter that spilled from her lips surprised her. Maybe that was what she needed, because the laughter also served as a cure of sorts. The crazy tilt her world had suffered these last few minutes disappeared as everything bounced back to the way it should be. She offered Mac a smile and lowered herself to the buttery-soft leather seat, sighing in appreciation at the warmth surrounding her.

Mac closed her door then moved around the front of the car, sliding into the driver's seat with a grace she had never noticed before. Or maybe she had noticed it and never truly appreciated it. Or maybe she had simply pushed it to the back of her mind, locking it away with the rest of her memories of him.

"Ready?" He tossed the question out, not waiting for an answer as he put the luxurious car in gear and moved down the long driveway.

Was she ready?

She had thought she was: ready for the night, ready for the chance to dig a little deeper, ready to learn something that would be useful.

And she was, as far as that went.

But was she ready for the resurgence of these old feelings and needs and wants? For the emotions she had ruthlessly pushed away for the last year?

Not even close.

chapter
THIRTEEN

Mac glanced at the GPS then deftly maneuvered the car to the exit ramp off 495. The weather here, just outside DC, was an annoying rain that would have turned 495 into a parking lot on any other night. But it was a holiday and the traffic, while still heavier than he had expected, was manageable.

He glanced at the GPS again then turned left at the light at the bottom of the ramp. They were entering an affluent section of Bethesda, filled with Georgian estates, old money, and even older power.

Mac stole a glance at his passenger, surprised at the physical blow he felt simply by looking at TR. He'd meant it when he told her she was beautiful, the thick words ripped from his throat before he could stop them.

But it was the truth. She *was* beautiful. He'd always thought so, even when she wore nothing more than jeans and sweater. Dressed as she was, in a shimmering gown that hugged every delicious curve of her body—she was more than beautiful. Her pale eyes, her wide smile, her infectious laughter and inner light—everything about her was beautiful.

But it was her hair that took his breath away, that robbed him of coherent thought and unleashed a desire he'd been trying to hide for too long.

Her thick hair was pulled up in a fancy knot at the back of her head that did nothing to contain the loose curls. They fell along her neck, framed her face, teased the curve of her jaw. Or maybe it had been styled that way on purpose. All he knew was that it took every ounce of self-control he possessed not to bury his hands into that thick hair, to pull those sparkling pins out one-by-one and watch as the luxurious strands fell over his hands, his wrists, his arms.

He yanked his gaze back to the road, taking a deep breath to control his wayward thoughts—thoughts he had no business thinking. He counted to three, slowly released his breath, then turned back to TR. "This is a pretty exclusive neighborhood. Who's hosting the party? I don't think you ever said."

TR shifted in her seat, one hand smoothing the silky fabric of her gown. "Um, a Senator."

"A Senator?" Mac let out a low whistle. "I'm impressed. How'd you manage to wrangle that invitation?"

"I honestly have no idea. And don't be impressed just yet. For all I know, they might show us to the servant's entrance when we get there."

Mac chuckled, started to reach over to give her shoulder a reassuring pat, changed his mind at the last second. Touching her wouldn't be smart, not now. Not when she was dressed like that, not while his hand was still burning from the brief contact against her bare skin when he'd placed his palm in the middle of her back earlier.

No touching. No thinking about touching. No thinking about anything, period. That was the only way he'd be able to survive tonight.

The GPS guided them off the main street and through the twists and turns of an older neighborhood, the large houses set farther apart, hidden behind stone walls and mature trees. Mac turned the luxury car—a loaner he was even more grateful for now—into a long driveway that curved in front of a stately Georgian estate before circling back on itself. Black-suited staff hovered nearby. One man approached the driver's door with an umbrella as Mac got out; he noticed another man doing the same for TR, holding out one gloved hand to assist her from the car as he held the umbrella protectively over her. He experienced a surprising urge to break the man's arms for simply touching TR and ruthlessly pushed it away. What the hell was his problem tonight? This sudden protectiveness, this need to keep TR close—it made no sense. Just like the hairs standing straight up on the back of his neck made no sense.

He moved closer to TR, took her hand and draped it through the crook of his arm as they were led inside. Another black-suited staffer asked for their names then directed them through a doorway into a large room that had been transformed into a luxurious oasis of gold and silver and black. Men in expensive tuxes guided jewel-studded women around the room. A trio of string musicians played from a small dais in the far corner of the room, the music soft enough that it didn't interfere with the hum of conversation filling the air.

TR stumbled, her hand tightening around his arm for a brief second as she quickly caught herself. She tilted her head up, her eyes wide and filled with surprise—and the smallest hint of anxiety.

"Why do I suddenly feel like an imposter?" The words were nothing more than a whisper, meant for his ears only. He placed one large hand over hers, gave it a small squeeze as he leaned down, ready to reassure her.

He stopped, the hairs on his neck prickling in warning as someone moved behind him. Close, too close. Mac stiffened, slowly pivoted as he carefully tucked TR behind him—and came face-to-face with one of the devil's minions.

"Sergeant...MacGregor, isn't it?" The Senator stopped a foot away, his broad smile at odds with the coolness permeating his shrewd hazel eyes. The man was in his sixties, his thick hair more silver than blonde. He was of average height and build, with nothing about his physical appearance to make him stand out. But it wasn't his physical appearance that had allowed him to climb to such a position of power in a city filled with powerful people. That steady climb came because of his intelligence, his ruthless drive—and his connections.

Mac quickly controlled his expression, hiding his anger, surprise, and distaste behind a mask of bored politeness. He accepted the Senator's hand for a brief shake and had to refrain from wiping his palm along his pants.

"It's *Mister*, not *Sergeant*. I'm retired now, sir." Which the son-of-a-bitch was well aware of.

"Ah, yes. Your accident. What a shame to end such a promising career." The Senator's gaze lingered on the scars covering the lower half of Mac's face then slid that same gaze to TR. The cool hazel eyes lit with appreciation as he reached for her hand and held it between both of his for longer than was polite. "Ms. Meyers. I'm delighted that you could make it. Such a pleasure to see you again."

"Thank you." TR tensed just the smallest bit as she pulled her hand from the Senator's and moved closer to Mac. "And thank you again for the invitation."

"Think nothing of it." The Senator's gaze moved from TR to Mac and back again. "I had no idea you and Mr. MacGregor were acquainted. How long have you known each other?"

Mac spoke quickly, stopping TR from answering. "We've only recently met. Through a mutual friend."

"How interesting." Something flashed in the Senator's eyes as his gaze met Mac's, something cold and calculating. He turned back to TR with a smile that oozed false charm. "I wanted to apologize again for the abruptness of our interview the other day."

"No apologies necessary, sir. I'm just grateful you were able to make some time for me, considering the time of year."

"Think nothing of it. Well, I've kept you two long enough." The Senator made a small motion with one hand, signaling for a nearby waiter. "Please, help yourself to some champagne. We'll be celebrating the new year soon."

Anger and suspicion burned in Mac's gut as he watched the Senator disappear into the crowd. He felt rather than heard TR's sigh of relief, saw her hand reach out to pluck a crystal flute from the serving tray of the hovering waiter.

Mac grabbed the glass from her hand, placed it

back on the tray, then led her toward a quiet corner. He leaned in close, his voice low and controlled as he spoke.

"TR, what the hell are you up to? Spill it. Now."

Chapter FOURTEEN

What the hell are you up to?

TR thought about playing dumb—for five seconds. It wasn't just the controlled anger burning in Mac's dark eyes, or the rigid way he held himself. He didn't frighten her—Mac would never hurt her, she knew that as surely as she knew her own name.

No, it wasn't Mac's reactions that convinced her playing dumb wasn't a smart move—it had been the interaction with the Senator. He'd made her feel...dirty. Contaminated. Confused. It was a completely different feeling from the other day. When she'd met the Senator in his office for the brief and essentially worthless interview, he'd been distracted and unfocused. It was almost as if she'd met two different men. The first one didn't impress her and the second one...the second one frightened her.

Beyond that was the astonishment that Mac knew the Senator. How? What kind of history was between them? Not a good one, that much was obvious. And the way the Senator had thrown that falsely sympathetic comment about the ending of Mac's career in his face, almost like he was gloating. It made no sense.

And neither did Mac's response when the Senator asked how long they'd known each other.

TR tilted her head back, curiosity filling her as she looked up at Mac. "Why did you tell the Senator we just met?"

"Because the less information he has, the better. Now tell me what's going on. What are you up to?"

"I'm not up to anything, Mac. I swear."

He was quiet for too long, watching her through narrowed eyes. He finally wrapped his hand around hers and tugged, guiding her away from the crowd that had moved closer. TR thought he was leading them to a secluded spot on the other side of the musicians but to her surprise, he led her out to the small dance floor. He pulled her into his arms, fitting her against his large body, and gently guided her in the steps of a slow dance.

"Mac. What—"

Mac dipped his head, his warm breath stirring the tendrils of hair curling around her ear. "He's watching. I need you to relax, pretend there's no place else you'd rather be right now than in my arms."

TR's steps faltered. *Pretend?* He thought she had to *pretend?* She took a deep breath and relaxed against him, followed him as he led her around the floor. She focused on a spot over his broad shoulder, afraid to meet his gaze, afraid he'd see the truth in her eyes.

His lips nuzzled her ear, sending shivers dancing along her spine. Except he wasn't nuzzling, he was whispering, his voice so low she could barely hear him.

"You came to DC to interview the Senator the other day."

It was a statement, not a question, but TR nodded her head anyway.

"Does this have anything to do with that story you're doing on the facility outside Frederick?"

TR nodded again, cleared her throat and tried to pitch her voice as low as Mac's. "Yes. He's the driving force behind it. There's concern about the land being historically significant but things are being pushed through so fast there's been no time for any in-depth studies."

Mac pulled away, his brows pulled low as he watched her. "You've got to be shitting me. *That's* what this is about? The fact that a piece of land might or might not have historical significance?"

"Yes. Mostly. I mean, it *was*."

The song drifted to an end. Mac led her off the floor, back to the far end of the room. He snagged two flutes of champagne from a passing waiter and offered one to her. Then he leaned closer, bracing one large arm against the wall behind her. To the casual observer, it would look as if they were nothing more than a pair of lovers having an intimate conversation.

Was that why he was standing so close? Close enough that his leg brushed against hers. Close enough that she was in danger of combusting from the heat radiating from his body.

TR took a small sip of the champagne, her gaze darting around the room, looking everywhere but at Mac. If she did, he'd see more than her bewilderment and confusion.

"What do you mean, *mostly* and it *was*? What's

going on?"

She hesitated, not sure how much to tell him. Would it hurt to tell him everything? About the email and that little nagging voice in her head that kept screaming something else was going on? She risked a glance at him, saw the hard set of his jaw, the fierce protectiveness flashing in his eyes.

She trusted him. She wouldn't have sought him out if she didn't, wouldn't have enlisted his unwitting assistance otherwise.

TR pulled her gaze from his and took a steadying breath. "I'm not sure what's going on, not really. This wasn't even supposed to be a big story, nothing more than a few column inches, if that. It still might not be."

"But?"

"But..." TR took another cleansing breath, released it in a quick sigh. "Two weeks ago, I received an email saying there was more to the complex and that I should look deeper."

Mac's gaze gave nothing away. "And?"

TR hesitated, wondering if she sounded as crazy as she thought. "And to follow the money. Follow my instinct."

"Do you know who sent the email?"

"No. I tried to send a reply but it bounced."

"And what does your instinct say?"

"I—I'm not sure. I think *something* is going on, I just don't know what. And..." She stopped, not sure how to explain. Mac's gentle voice urged her on so she took a quick breath and continued. "There was something off about the Senator the other day. During our interview."

"Yeah, I bet there was. The man's a slime ball."

"No, not that. Mac, he was like a different person

than the man who was just talking to us. He was confused. Distracted. It was like he wasn't sure where he was or what I was even doing there. He kept repeating himself and half of what he said didn't even make sense."

Mac's gaze turned thoughtful and for a long minute, he said nothing. He looked around the room, taking in everything and nothing, then turned back to her. "Don't trust him, TR—"

"I don't."

"And stay away from him whenever possible." Mac held up his hand, stopping her complaint before she could even form the words. "I know this involves work and that might not be possible. But if you need to meet with him again, make sure someone is with you. Trust me, if the Senator is involved, there's definitely something going on. And whatever it is, it isn't good."

"How do you know him?"

Mac's gaze briefly darted away, but not before she saw the anger in his eyes. "Long story."

She thought about pushing, immediately decided against it. There was a finality in his words, in the tone of his voice, that let her know he wouldn't discuss it. Not now. Maybe not ever.

He turned back to her, his dark gaze penetrating, seeking. "How'd you manage an invitation here tonight?"

"I don't know. It showed up about a week after the email."

"And you didn't think that was suspicious at all?"

TR laughed, the brief sound escaping her on a whisper. "Of course, I did. Look around, Mac. This isn't exactly a crowd I'm part of. And I'm not seeing any other reporters, especially any from a weekly regional paper that doesn't even register on DC's blip."

"But you came anyway."

"I had to. It was too big an opportunity to pass up. Especially if I got the chance..." Her voice trailed off and she quickly looked away, her face heating under Mac's scrutiny. Would he notice? Would he be able to finish her thought and figure out what she had planned?

If the sudden tensing of his body wasn't answer enough, his soft swearing certainly was.

"I don't believe it. Christ. TR, please tell me you weren't planning on snooping around."

"I—"

"Of all the—" Mac swore again. "You wouldn't have gotten more than three feet in any direction outside of this room without someone following you."

"I thought that maybe—I mean, if I had someone to distract—"

"Is that where I was supposed to come in?" There was something in Mac's voice—a tightness, a bitterness—that made her look up. His dark eyes were unreadable, his face eerily blank. "Have the scarred monster scare everyone so they wouldn't notice you slinking around where you don't belong?"

Anger exploded through her, surprising in its swiftness. "Stop it. Just—stop it."

"Why? We both know it's true."

"Bullshit!" The sharp word came out in a hiss, silencing Mac and startling her. She took a deep breath, fighting for a semblance of control, fighting to keep the words inside. But she couldn't, not anymore, not when Mac was staring at her the way he was, like he was convinced that the marks on his face were the only things that defined him.

"You don't get it. You never have." She raised her hand, her heart squeezing when she noticed Mac's brief flinch a second before she rested her palm against his jaw. He stiffened under her touch, tried to pull away, but she held him in place with nothing more than the force of her gaze.

Slowly, her touch light and gentle, she traced the scars with the tip of her finger. The long one that ran from the corner of his mouth to each edge of his jaw, the jagged flesh oddly smooth. The shorter ones, twisted and knotted, that bisected the large one. Even the faint lines that cut across his chin.

Mac reached for her hand, his fingers closing around her wrist. Rough, strong—but gentle, too. He didn't move her hand as she expected. He didn't do anything except watch her.

"TR—"

"I don't care about these, Mac. I never have. They don't make you who you are. They don't define you." TR lowered her hand, dragging his with it. She traced the edge of the crisp white shirt down to the center of his chest, placed her palm over the steady beating of his heart. "*This* is what I care about."

She stepped toward him, her breasts brushing against the firm expanse of his chest. Then she pressed her mouth to his, the kiss soft and lingering yet over too soon as she pulled away.

"We should get something to eat before we leave."

Chapter FIFTEEN

This is what I care about.

TR's words had thrown him off-balance. Even now, more than three hours later, he could still feel the heat of her palm pressed against the middle of his chest. Could still hear the soft conviction of her voice.

Could still see the naked desire in her clear eyes.

Off-balance? No, she'd done more than simply throw him off-balance. Christ, it was a fucking miracle he could still walk and breathe at the same time.

Mac's gaze swept the room, immediately finding her. She was twenty feet away, deep in animated conversation with a Congresswoman and a lobbyist, talking about who knew what. For someone who had been convinced she didn't fit in with this crowd, she was certainly making a fair amount of new acquaintances.

He let his gaze linger on TR for a few seconds longer then looked around the room. Slow, casual, as if he was nothing more than a curious guest. The Senator was near the center of the room, speaking with two men he didn't recognize.

Mac wondered again about his decision to stay, worried that it had been the wrong one.

No. As uncomfortable as the Senator made him, it was better that they had stayed. Leaving so soon after getting here would have raised suspicions. As long as the Senator remained in sight, Mac was comfortable with staying—especially since TR had abandoned her half-baked plan of snooping around.

Mac glanced at his watch. The New Year would be here in two more minutes. They could leave after the celebration.

He accepted two glasses of champagne from the passing waiter and made his way over to TR. She turned, her mouth curling into a smile when he approached. He told himself not to read into her smile or the glimmer of appreciation dancing in her eyes. Told himself not to read into the way she stepped closer and placed her hand on his arm.

Excitement filled the air, disbanding the slight stuffiness that had hovered over the room just a few minutes earlier. The Senator was standing near the musicians now, directing everyone's attention to the large television that had appeared thirty minutes earlier. The screen showed a massive crowd huddled together in Times Square before moving to the large ball making its slow descent.

Mac didn't give a shit about the crowd or the brightly-lit ball. The only thing he cared about was the woman by his side, her head tilted back as she gazed into his eyes, a soft smile lighting her face.

The crowd in the room started counting down in

time with the television.

Ten.

Someone jostled TR from behind and she stumbled against him. Her face heated with a pale blush but she didn't pull away.

Nine.

Mac wrapped his arm around her waist and pulled her closer. Could she feel the heavy beating of his heart? She must, with her hand pressed against his chest that way.

Eight.

Her eyes widened, desire flaring in their pale blue depths when his gaze caught hers.

Seven.

Her mouth parted, her tongue darting out to sweep along the plumpness of her lower lip. Mac followed the movement with his eyes, hunger welling deep inside him.

Six.

TR leaned even closer, her body shuddering with a shaky breath when he ran one rough hand down her arm.

Five.

She opened her mouth, whispered his name in a breath so soft, there was no way he should be able to hear it. But he did. Or maybe he didn't, maybe he simply felt it.

Four.

He dragged his hand up her arm, her skin pebbling under his touch. Her lids fluttered closed as he wrapped his hand behind her neck, his fingers tangling in the thickness of her soft hair.

Three.

Her eyes opened, her gaze filled with warmth and

need as he dipped his head toward hers.

Two.

She draped her arms around his neck, reaching up to meet him. A whisper of breath escaped her, brushing against his lips in a soft caress.

One.

Mac's mouth closed over hers. Soft, hesitant at first. Learning. Tasting. Teasing. But it wasn't enough. It would never be enough.

TR pressed herself closer, a whisper of need escaping from her mouth and into his. He cupped her face between his palms, the cool smoothness of her skin acting like a balm to his battered soul. He titled his head and deepened the kiss, drinking in the sweet nectar of TR's mouth as fires of need raged through him.

Scorching. Cleansing.

Consuming.

There was nothing else around them. No cheering crowd. No cries of *Happy New Year*. No clinking of crystal against crystal.

There was only TR, her soft curves pressed against him as he lost himself in her touch, her taste, her scent.

Her kiss.

And the man stood in the shadows, watching.

Waiting.

~ Not *Quite* The End ~

THE PROTECTOR: MAC
COVER SIX SECURITY BOOK 2

These men never back away from danger—and always fall hard for love in *Cover Six Security*, an explosive new series from USA Today Bestselling Author Lisa B. Kamps

Gordon "Mac" MacGregor swore an oath to protect and defend—an oath he continues to uphold as a former Army Ranger specializing in dark ops private security with Cover Six Security. Danger is a constant companion—and one of the few things that make him feel alive. He doesn't expect that danger to come in the form of the Tabitha "TR" Meyers, the only woman who sees him for who he truly is—and the only woman he's ever sworn off.

TR rarely abides by the rules, not when there's something she needs—and right now, she needs Mac. She enlists his help for one night, thinking she can simply walk away when it's over. But that one night is just the beginning, thrusting both of them into a dangerous web of scandal and cover-up with roots that run deeper than either of them expects.

When TR becomes an unwitting pawn in a game of deception and revenge, Mac will do anything to protect her—even if it means risking his own heart.

Turn the page for exciting peek at *The Protector: MAC,* **the continuation of Mac and TR's story and the launch title in the explosive new series,** *Cover Six Security.*

Lisa B. Kamps

The kiss caught her by surprise. Soft, hesitant at first. Learning. Tasting. Teasing. But it wasn't enough. It could never be enough.

She pressed herself closer, a whisper of need escaping her. He cupped her face between his rough palms and deepened the kiss. Drinking her in. Unleashing fires of need kept banked for too long.

Scorching. Cleansing. Deep and intense. God, so intense. All she wanted to do was crawl on top of Mac, crawl inside *him, be consumed by him, the crowd be damned. He was everything she wanted*—needed. *Hot. Hard.*

And his mouth. God, his mouth. So deceptively soft. Gentle. And hot. So hot—

Cold.

So painfully cold, a hundred thousand needles pricking her skin. *Under* her skin, down to bone and marrow. Shredding. Tearing. Ripping.

Consciousness returned slowly. Disoriented, sluggish, confused. Something was wrong, she shouldn't be this cold. Where was Mac? He was gone, his heat replaced by the shocking iciness surrounding her. She needed him, needed his heat—

Water pooled around her feet, her legs, her hips. She was entrenched in a dreamlike state. There was no sound other than the oddly hollow gurgle of water as it washed around her. No illumination other than the pale ghostly hue of the dashboard lights wavering through the watery darkness surrounding her. And cold, so bitterly cold. Freezing. Numbing.

She watched, detached, as her hands floated near the deflated bag hanging from the steering wheel. Struggled to make sense of everything, knowing something was wrong.

Something—

Full consciousness returned and with it, fear. Raw, consuming. Terrifying. Panic ripped through her as she struggled with the seatbelt, her numb fingers useless. The water was higher now, to her chest, coming in faster as the car descended deeper into murky blackness.

She needed to get out. *Now*. But she was trapped by the seatbelt, couldn't get it to release. Couldn't open the door—

Oh God, no.

No!

The sound of her harsh breathing echoed around her, sharp and terrified. Shallow. Fast. *Too* fast, she was hyperventilating, on the verge of passing out.

On the verge of drowning.

The water climbed even higher. Past her chest. Her shoulders. Biting cold, sapping what little strength she had, increasing the panic and desperation clawing at her. She struggled with the seatbelt, fought to control her breathing, fought to get free—

But it was too late.

One breath. One more, dark water rushing over her face, into her mouth, her nose.

Too late—

Mac—

THE GUARDIAN: DARYL
COVER SIX SECURITY BOOK 2

These men never back away from danger—and always fall hard for love in *Cover Six Security*, an explosive new series from *USA Today* Bestselling Author Lisa B. Kamps

Daryl "Zeus" Anderson walks the edge of danger. Strong. Dependable. Always in control--except for that one night in a tropical paradise that still haunts him. When an old friend calls in a favor, Daryl answers the call, never expecting to come face-to-face with the woman who damn near shattered his restraint--and his heart.

Kelsey Davis has been running for the last five years: for her safety, for her sanity, for more than just her life. The dangerous game she's been thrust into is nearing an end and she's forced to turn to the man her father swears will guard her with his life--the same man she's already run away from once.

The clock is ticking and Kelsey needs to decide if she can trust her new guardian with more than her heart. Because in this game, there's more at stake than love-- and making the wrong decision could cost much more than just their lives.

Don't miss the next sizzling title in the Cover Six Security series, *The Guardian: DARYL*, now available.

THE DEFENDER: RYDER
COVER SIX SECURITY BOOK 3

These men never back away from danger—and always fall hard for love in *Cover Six Security,* an explosive new series from *USA Today* Bestselling Author Lisa B. Kamps

Ryder "Boomer" Hess: former Army Ranger. Demolitions expert. Problem solver...and the unluckiest bastard around when it comes to love. Meeting women is never a problem but actually surviving a relationship? Not happening. And all because of his kid sister's best friend.

Hannah Montgomery: professional volunteer. Humanitarian activist. Eternal optimist...and a woman who lost her heart years ago to her best friend's brother. She's learned to turn that heartache into something useful and now loses herself in helping others...until *he* shows up and turns her world upside down.

When Ryder gets a call that his sister—and Hannah—could be in trouble, he drops everything and rushes to their rescue—and quickly learns that he might be the one who needs rescuing the most. But danger of another sort looms on the horizon and it's up to Ryder to save them. And if he fails, he'll lose a lot more than just his heart this time.

Don't miss the third sizzling title in the Cover Six Security series, *The Defender: RYDER*, now available.

About the AUTHOR

Lisa B. Kamps is a *USA Today* Bestselling Author who writes steamy romance with real-life characters and relatable stories that evoke deep emotion. She likes her men hard, her bed soft, her coffee strong, her whiskey neat, and her wine chilled...and when it comes to sports, hockey is the only thing that matters!

Lisa currently lives in Maryland with her husband and two sons (who are mostly sorta-kinda out of the house), one very spoiled Border Collie, two cats with major attitude, several head of cattle, and entirely too many chickens to count. When she's not busy writing or chasing animals, she's cheering loudly for her favorite hockey team, the Washington Capitals--or going through withdrawal and waiting for October to roll back around!

Website: www.LisaBKamps.com
Newsletter: http://www.lisabkamps.com/signup/
Email: LisaBKamps@gmail.com
Facebook:
https://www.facebook.com/authorLisaBKamps
Kamps Korner Facebook Group:
https://www.facebook.com/groups/1160217000707067/
BookBub:
https://www.bookbub.com/authors/lisa-b-kamps

Goodreads: https://www.goodreads.com/LBKamps
Instagram: https://www.instagram.com/lbkamps/
Twitter: https://twitter.com/LBKamps
Amazon Author Page:
http://www.amazon.com/author/lisabkamps